K L   F
                                    GOR

This book is d  wn below.

22 JUN 20

D0766275

Ed Gorman

A Cry of Shadows

A Jack Dwyer Mystery

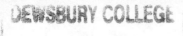
This edition published in 1999 by
Allison & Busby Limited
114 New Cavendish Street
London W1M 7FD
http://www.allisonandbusby.ltd.uk

First published in the USA in 1990 by St Martin's Press

A catalogue record for this book is available from the British Library

ISBN 0 74900 411 8

Printed by Biddles Ltd, Guildford, Surrey

In memory of my good friend Doc

Acknowledgments

Three people helped me by reading the first draft of this manuscript and making many valuable suggestions— Marcia Muller, Bill Pronzini and Barb Kramer. Thank you, folks.

E. G.

About suffering they were never wrong,
The Old Masters: how well they understood
Its human position; how it takes place
While someone else is eating or opening a window
    or just walking dully along . . .
        —W. H. Auden, "Musée des Beaux Arts"

1

There were at least 2,341 other things I wanted to be doing that December morning. Tramping around a dirty alley in fifteen-below temperature was not one of them.

The alley lay behind the Avanti, the sort of chic restaurant where BMWs just naturally go of their own volition, not unlike homing pigeons, and where a midwesterner like myself can pronounce no more than three of the items on the menu.

The backs of the buildings ran to two stories and dirty brick. Near the rear stoops were Dumpsters and garbage cans with all the attendant scrawny dogs and cats prowling for sustenance. Earlier I'd seen a freezing tiny tabby female. I'd picked her up and put her in my overcoat pocket so she could get warm for at least a while. Even beneath my lined gloves I could feel her frail ribs tremble with cold. I carried her around and every once in a while she'd poke her head up and look at me with those sweet little eyes, but then she started clawing in such a way that I thought she might need to pee. So I set her down and damned if she didn't immediately lift her cute little tail and make a small clump of snow corn yellow. Then she bounded off and I wondered if I maybe shouldn't have taken her home. Donna Harris, the woman I see, was

gone a week on a skiing trip with advertising people and I was in need of company. But the tabby
was gone before I could make up my mind. In some
peculiar way, I felt jilted by the kitty, which should
tell you something about the state of my self-esteem.

I had no idea what I was looking for. One of the
Avanti's three owners, a rather imperious blond
man named Richard Coburn, had simply told me
that the place had been having "some trouble" and
wanted me to check the alley to see if there was
any way that anybody could get into the rear of
the place without a key.

The first thing I checked was the restaurant's
back doors. One of them was a typical steel FIRE
EXIT setup, with a nonfunctioning knob outside and
an inside knob that would trigger a fire alarm. The
other door was an employee entrance and its outside knob was always locked. You had to ring a
buzzer to be let in. Deliveries also came through
this door. All delivery personnel had to sign in and
out and a restaurant employee was supposed to be
with them at all times. The inside knob was always
left unlocked in case of emergencies. City fire codes
mandated this.

On either side of the two doors, and up four
feet, were windows covered with wire mesh. I
dragged a crate over and checked each grid of
mesh. Tight, secure. No evidence of tampering.

So I started roaming the alley, which was where
I found the tabby and which was also where I found
the priest rooting through the garbage can.

By this time I was pretty cold. I clapped my hands together. I covered my running nose with one of my black-gloved hands. I cupped my gloves sea-shell-like over my ears. About all I could do with my toes was wriggle them and make sure they hadn't frozen off. Vanity notwithstanding, I decided then and there—rather in the way a drunk takes an oath of sobriety—to start wearing woolen socks and long underwear. It was time I start taking a few fashion risks, anyway. Donna always joked that I looked like a floorwalker in the men's fashion section of K-Mart.

The priest wore no coat, just his short-sleeved cleric's shirt and Roman collar. I didn't think he was a priest, but then I didn't have any idea what he might really be. He stood over a garbage can, eating a scrawny chicken leg he'd just plucked from inside. He ate with a frenzied, feral quality that was ugly to see, like stumbling on the sight of somebody's darkest sexual secret. He was my height, perhaps six feet, and slender. He was probably in his sixties. He was sleekly bald with little fringes of gray hair riding above small pink ears. If he was freezing—and he had to be—he didn't let on.

He ate the dirty chicken leg with relish. When he was finished, he dropped the bone and gristle back into the garbage can. He bent over and was about to root around for another delicacy when he sensed me.

He stopped in midmotion, not looking up yet, but preparing himself. I was no more than ten feet away. I could see the long muscles in his neck tense. I assumed he was going to raise his head, confirm my presence, and then take off, scared. Snow blew grainy against my face, flying up the rusty iron fire escapes on the buildings.

He raised his head. The madness of his blue eyes was unfathomable. Pain, rage, and lunacy lay behind his blue blue gaze. His voice surprised me. It was a good, steady, appealing bass. No frenzy in it whatsoever. He said, " 'I am the bread of life; he who comes to me shall not hunger.' Do you know who said that, traveler?"

"Jesus said that."

"Were you raised to believe in Jesus?"

"Yes, I was."

"Have you deserted his teachings?"

I nodded to his arms. "Do you know there's a shelter two blocks from here?"

He smiled with stubby gray teeth long in need of a dentist. " 'But they flattered him with their mouths; they lied to him with their tongues. Their heart was not steadfast toward him; they were not true to his convenant.' That is the shelter."

"They'd give you clothes. And some food."

He fixed me with his sad crazed gaze. "They feed the body, traveler. They do not feed the soul."

The priest saw him first, coming up behind me. All I heard were running feet crunching through the snow.

By the time Richard Coburn came abreast of me, a terrible fear was in the priest's eyes and he was already turning from the garbage can and starting to run away to the other end of the alley. He looked almost comic, sliding and slipping on the icy snow, a scarecrow of a man.

"You sonofabitch! You get away from my place and you stay away!" Coburn shouted to the retreating man.

By the time Coburn reached me, the freezing air was laden with his cologne and his hot quick rage. I saw now why the derelict had been so frightened. Coburn carried a tidy .45 jammed into his fist. He waved it in the air as he passed me and ran down the alley after the priest.

"You sonofabitch!" Coburn kept shouting. "You sonofabitch!"

The derelict disappeared around the corner. Coburn quit running. He turned back around, panting heavily, and came back up to me. Handsome and sleek as he was, he was still thirty pounds overweight and this kind of anger and exertion had spent him. "That sonofabitch," he kept saying in gasps. "That sonofabitch."

2

"You ever work in a restaurant, Dwyer?"

"Yeah."

"It's a bitch."

"I know."

"If you've got an upscale demographic, as we do here, then you've got to constantly be kissing the customers' asses. They are all of the opinion that they deserve the kind of service enjoyed by popes and rajahs. You know?"

"I know."

"We used to have a rich woman who wore a ratty fox stole and walked with a cane because of arthritis and every night she'd drink three martinis, she'd pick a fight with me about this fly in her water glass. She'd always demand a new glass of water."

I said, "Of course there was no fly in her glass."

He laughed. "Then you know what I'm talking about."

In fact, my busboy days in high school were some of my worst memories. If the maitre d' wasn't gnawing on you for giving vile offense to this or that customer, then the head-waiter was stealing your share of the tips. Plus I wasn't exactly graceful. I must have dropped at least as many dishes as I'd bused. Combat soldiers couldn't have had a much higher stress level. Finally, I quit and took a graveyard-shift gig at a Shell station. That way all I had to worry about were teenagers with guns who wanted my money.

Coburn said, sighing, "We've got one real sweetheart here. Tim, this stockbroker who's a real punk. He always gets drunk and hits on the waitresses. He more or less raped one of them out in the alley one night."

"More or less?"

"She agreed to accept a car for not pressing charges."

"He still come in?"

"Oh, sure. He'll probably be in tonight."

"Why not throw him out?"

"Can't."

"It's your place."

"He's too important."

"Ah."

"Some day I'm going to take the kid and pound the hell out of his face. Maybe in the next couple of weeks. As a Christmas present to myself."

He picked up his glass. He killed it off in a swig. It was rye and water, heavy on the former. It was also 10:34 A.M. But I was raised to believe that a man's problems are his own unless he pays you to do something about them.

"So what did you find out in the alley?"

"Not much."

"No sign of anybody breaking in?"

"None." I paused. "You ever going to tell me what's going on here?"

He stared at me. He was a big man in all respects. In his brown turtleneck and Harris tweed jacket, he seemed even bigger, like a professional wrestler tamed and groomed to greet people politely. "Just having a few problems is all."

"Anything American Security can help you with?"

"You trying to drum up business?" Every other line or so, he sounded angry. Somewhere in there was disappointment, too, as if at some point in his life he'd had big hopes for the world and it had let him down pretty badly.

"Sure. Everybody needs business."

That made him smile. "Just some bullshit is all. Going on here, I mean."

"That's pretty vague."

He wasn't paying attention anymore. He slammed down his empty glass and shouted, "Can't you see what the hell you're doing to that floor, Earle?"

He was addressing a young black kid, maybe eighteen, who was carrying a stack of chairs across a small dance floor. The kid had mud on his shoes. Goopy dark tracks marked his passage. The kid reminded me of me in my busboy days.

"Oh, God, Mr. Coburn, I'm sorry," the kid said. "I'll go get a mop and clean it up right away."

Christ on the cross couldn't have looked any more miserable.

"I'm surrounded by idiots," Coburn said, self-pity and anger keeping his voice loud enough for the kid to hear him.

The kid disappeared. Coburn dropped his head momentarily. He seemed to be doing some kind of deep-breathing exercises. Getting back in control. Then he raised his head and raised his glass. A very pretty lady bartender nodded to him. She had been watching it all. She seemed neither shocked nor upset by his outburst. Just weary.

"Sometimes I wonder if all the bullshit's worth it, you know?" he said to me while he waited for his drink. Despite his size and his formidable rage, he sounded like a youngster.

The bartender brought the drink over on an elegant seashell tray. She set it down in front of him with a great air of formality. She picked up the glass he'd just finished with. This drink looked even meaner than the last. She glanced at me. She had intelligent brown eyes and a sad sweet face. There was an air of irony about her, as if she had seen enough to know that little of it was worth any personal grief. She carried an extra fifteen pounds with erotic elegance. In her white blouse and black slacks, she looked newly showered and fresh. She had radiant, thick dark hair that tumbled to frail shoulders. She smelled wonderful.

She said, very quietly, "You wanted me to count them off."

Instead of getting angry, Richard Coburn sighed. His shoulders sagged. "I know how many it is." He stared at the drink. "Three."

"Three," she said, and the way she said it, resigned but concerned, made me wonder if she might be more to Coburn than simply an employee. "Why don't you have some coffee to go with it?"

He patted her hand. "Maybe next round."

She looked at me. Obviously I was an intruder. Obviously she wanted to say something private to him. She decided to say it. "That means you're planning on a next round?"

I stood up. "I think I'll find the men's room."

Coburn didn't try to stop me. He just kept staring at the woman. It wasn't a difficult task.

Nothing is lonelier than a shut-down restaurant. Fine as this one was, now there was something tawdry and melancholy about it, with all the chairs and tables stacked and cleaning people moving up and down the aisles. Without the glow of nighttime lights, you could see where the flocked wallpaper was starting to unravel in places, where smoke had stained some of the heavy white curtains on the west wall, where a mercury crack snaked down one of the full-length mirrors.

The bathroom was big and white and newly tiled. It was an ideal place for people to do cocaine while checking out their tuxedos in the mirror. I used a urinal clean enough to eat off, not that I'd want to try. In a square of window above a vent shaft I saw the slate gray, overcast sky. Fifty below with the wind chill factor. I thought of the crazed priest again. No coat. I also thought of how angry Coburn had been when he'd seen him. Irrationally angry, really.

When I got back to Coburn's table, the bartender

was gone and in her place was a different type of beautiful lady, a cold beauty who inspired fear as much as desire. She was tall, blond, dressed in a tailored gray suit. She was every Japanese businessman's American wet dream.

Just as I reached the table, she leaned into Coburn and slapped him. She slapped him very hard. His head jerked back and for a moment, stunned, his eyes went shut.

Apparently, I'd come back a few minutes too early.

I stood at the table not knowing what to do.

Coburn, eyes opened again, surprised me by laughing. It was quite a hearty laugh, and every bit as loud in the morning silence as the slap had been. The lady bartender was back behind the bar again, cleaning glasses and watching intently. Coburn said, "Dwyer, this is my wife, Deirdre."

Having absolutely no idea of what etiquette called for at a moment like this, I mouthed my usual inappropriate remark. "Nice to meet you, Mrs. Coburn."

She glared at me. "Who's he?"

"A private investigator."

"Ducky. Just fucking ducky. And what are we doing with a private investigator?"

Coburn looked nervous. He also looked as if he'd forgotten all about being slapped. Maybe it was something that happened frequently. "We'll talk about it later."

I'd been engrossed enough in the melodrama

that I hadn't noticed the new man appear. He wore a blue double-breasted suit, a very white shirt, a very red tie, and dark hair slicked back with so much grease he might have been a gigolo in a Cole Porter musical. He was tanned, he was trim, and he was obviously displeased with everything he saw.

"I don't give a damn what you two do in private," he said. "But I resent you doing it in a place I own a full third of." He glared at Coburn and said, "And just what the hell are we doing with a private investigator here, Richard?"

Coburn nervously introduced the man as his partner, Tom Anton, then started to say something in his own defense but Anton didn't let him. "I want this guy out of here. Now."

This was Coburn's morning for getting ultimatums. He sat there squirming, this big forlorn guy whose only real weapons were his fists.

He said, in a croaking voice, "Maybe it would be better if you left, Dwyer. Just send me a bill."

His partner, glossy and enraged, said, "I want to know what the hell he's doing here in the first place."

"Just send me a bill, Dwyer," Coburn said. "All right?" He sounded miserable.

I nodded, glanced at the beautiful wife and the handsome partner, feeling shabby and a little sweaty by contrast, and then left.

On my way out, I ran into Earle, the black kid who'd been tracking up the dance floor. He said, "They're crazy in this place, you know that?"

I grinned. "Yeah, that's just what I was starting to think."

He grinned back.

3

Two mornings later, so early and so cold the solitary window of my apartment was silver blue with frost, I rolled out of the cocoon of the covers, reached up with a naked, hairy arm and grabbed the telephone that was performing with such aggravating urgency.

"Dwyer?"

"Umm-hmmphf."

"You're still asleep, aren't you?"

"Was asleep. Past tense."

"Do you know who this is?"

"Of course I do."

"I mean, I know it's your day off but I thought I'd better call you anyway."

It's difficult to dislike Bobby Lee. A bottle blonde who still affects something resembling a beehive, a woman of small but substantive sweet charms and an enormous chest usually swathed in T-shirts bearing the visage of popular country-western stars, a curiously prim Southern Baptist who will laugh at a joke she considers "naughty" but literally cry if you use the F-word in front of her ("You have no respect for women," she once furiously told our boss)—Bobby Lee is the closest thing I have to a real friend at the American Security Agency.

I got up and reached for a cigarette. Reflex. I'd

given up devil weeds three years earlier. I think I was still mad about it.

"What's up?" I asked.

"You know that restaurant you went to the other day to check out the security system?"

"Right."

"Wasn't that guy's name Coburn?"

"Right. Richard Coburn."

"Somebody murdered him."

"Huh?"

"Last night."

"They're sure it was murder?"

"Shot in the back in the parking lot while he was getting into his car."

"Have they arrested anybody yet?"

"Not yet." Pause. "Maybe you should call your detective friend Edelman at the police station."

"What would I tell him?"

"Maybe you know more than you think?"

I laughed. "With me, it's always the other way around, Bobby Lee. I know much less than I think."

She giggled. "I won't give you an argument there."

"God," I said, trying to imagine the big, angry man dead. I'll bet it took him a while to die. I'll bet he didn't die easily, either. "In the parking lot."

"In the back."

"God," I said again, and thought of the woman slapping him.

"Well," Bobby Lee said, "I just thought I'd tell you. What made me think of it was that your time sheet came across my desk this morning. It had his name on it for billing."

"Thanks for telling me."

"What're you going to do today?"

"Some Christmas shopping, I guess. And Chrissie's supposed to call me today."

"Well, have a nice time."

My son and daughter—Rob and Chrissie—are seventeen and fifteen respectively. Both are in high school, both have long since adjusted to the divorce that brought them a new stepfather (actually not a bad guy despite my first impressions), and both make the same effort to remember my birthday as I to remember theirs. While it's not an ideal situation—I've always wondered if their mother and I tried hard enough to make the marriage work—we love and respect each other, and are genuinely interested in each other, and hearing from either or both of them always has a way of making even a glum day better.

Half an hour after Bobby Lee's call, I was in the bathroom shaving when the phone rang. Towel around my widening middle, I went out to the living room and picked up the phone, laying a few inches of foamy white shaving soap along the black receiver.

"Hi, Dad. Calling at a bad time?"

"Not at all, Chrissie."

"So how are things going?"

"Pretty good."

"How's Donna?"

"Out of town is how Donna is."

"You miss her?"

"Sure."

"She's nice. I like her"

"I know you do and I appreciate that." Pause. "But why do I have the feeling that we're not really talking about what you want to talk about?"

"God, Dad. ESP." She laughed. "It's the cake."

"Cake?"

"I was baking you this birthday cake as a surprise. Just kind of experimenting before I made you the real one."

"Oh, sweetheart. You don't need to go to all that trouble."

Pause. "It didn't turn out so well." Pause. "Actually, it's the worst cake I've ever seen or tasted. Kenny wouldn't even eat it." Kenny is their collie, notorious for eating whatever you put in front of him.

"So Rob's going to make you one," she said. "He's actually much better in the kitchen than I am."

"That's all right, honey. You're a lot better at history than he is."

"Yeah, and that really came in handy while I was making your cake." She laughed. "Maybe I'll be better when I take home ec next year. That's why Rob's so good. He took home ec last year."

"Are we still going to the movie next week?"

"God, I hope so. I've been planning on it all

month." When she was a little girl, I took her and Rob without fail to *The Lady and the Tramp* every Christmastime. These days, I took Rob to his own type of holiday movie—usually a *Star Trek* or some other action movie—but I took my little girl to *Lady*.

"Don't worry about the cake, hon. You'll get better at baking. You'll see."

Rob grabbed the phone then and said, "Wait'll you taste mine, Dad! Mine can actually be ingested by human beings!"

I heard them wrestling around for the receiver and then Chrissie, triumphant, said into the phone, "I'm glad one of us is mature around here, aren't you, Dad?"

She said a few more things about school and we hung up.

4

I wore Reeboks and I wore my long underwear because the big glass doors at the front of the Quality Mart Discount Store were always opening and closing and I wore my only good tweed jacket and the blue oxford button-down shirt Chrissie bought me a few months ago. Chrissie and Rob were now two days gone on their skiing trip and I wanted badly to talk to them, not to interrupt their lives in any way, just to say hi and tell them that I missed them and that I loved them. Maybe Calvin Conway, the feckless sneak thief I'd busted half an hour earlier, was right. Maybe this eighteen-shopping-days-before-Christmas jazz was getting to me after all.

There was no employee lunchroom at Quality Mart. You ate in the tiny "restaurant" that smelled of grease and seemed to be populated almost exclusively by overweight ethnic grandmas made even stockier by their bulky winter coats and all their GI Joe and Barbie-and-Ken-doll packages. These were the women you saw at the drunkard's mass, the early one before first light, and most of them were long widowed and bereft of children except for mandatory holiday calls and you wondered what they did with themselves all day and what if any were their joys and you hated yourself for feeling superior to them when they in fact knew what mattered and you probably didn't know at all.

She was waiting for me in a booth next to a big gaudy sign that advertised corn dogs. I recognized her immediately. She was even more beautiful than I recalled and I found myself disliking her just as much.

She watched me walk over to her.

"I called your company and badgered them into telling me where I'd find you. I finally told them that I planned to spend a lot of money with them and they relented. I hope you don't mind."

"I'm sorry about your husband."

"Yes. Aren't we all?"

I wasn't sure how to respond. Most wives don't make sarcastic remarks about husbands three days dead. I shook my head and said, "You're a peach, Mrs. Coburn."

She frowned. "The police have a suspect, in case you're interested. A black boy named Earle. He didn't do it." Then, "Are you going to sit down, Mr. Dwyer?"

I sat down. When the waitress came I ordered a cheeseburger and fries and a Diet Pepsi. When she went away, the bereaved widow said, "Did you see her sweat?"

"It's hot in here. Plus it's packed and she's busy. And she's probably working for minimum wage and worrying about her three kids at home." I shook my head. "Jesus."

"Is it asking too much that people stay *dry* while they're serving me?"

"How nice for you," I said. "To live in a universe where people who work hard don't sweat."

She stared at me. Much as I disliked her, I couldn't help but note again how lovely she looked in her wine-colored turtleneck and brown suede car coat, with her tumbling blond hair and her full, cruel, erotic mouth. She was the prize all the rich boys would lay their lives down trying to win.

She said, "If I eat a corn dog, will you like me any better?"

"Maybe."

"It's worth a try, then."

So she had a corn dog. She ate it tentatively, as if afraid to know what might be inside.

"This is ducky," she said, her cute little white teeth soiled with flecks of corn dog.

"I heard they make them with real dogs," I said.

She said, "This must he a Pekingese. Very tough." After another bite, "Don't you think I'm trying hard to be a good sport?"

"A veritable saint."

"Do you really hate me all that much?"

"Probably not all that much."

"Then why don't we try to be pleasant with each other?"

"Pleasant it is, then."

"Really, Mr. Dwyer?"

"Really."

She said, "I notice you're not eating a corn dog."

"You think I'd eat something like that?"

She smiled. "I'll bet you raised your share of hell when you were a boy."

"I sure tried."

"You were probably one of those boys from the West Side who always tried to get my attention at the movie theater on Saturday afternoons."

"John Agar double features."

"Really. I could never figure that out. If they wanted me to be nice to them, why weren't they nice to me?"

I shrugged. "You probably scared them."

"But I was a girl."

"Doesn't matter. In fact, the scariest people I knew growing up were girls. Nothing can intimidate you like beauty."

"Really?" she said around her corn dog. "I'm learning some things here today, aren't I?"

I leaned forward. "Who are you betting on, Mrs. Coburn?"

She set the corn dog down and finished swallowing and said, "Do you mean who do I think killed Richard?"

"Right."

"I'm not sure. I just know it wasn't Earle." She put her head down and stared at the remains of her corn dog. She lifted her head and said, "Something you said a little while ago really pissed me off."

"I see."

"Don't you even want to know what it was?"

"I suppose when I said you were a peach."

She was angry. She calmed herself enough to speak. "I'm not a 'peach,' Mr. Dwyer. We didn't have a good marriage and it wasn't my fault. I only went to bed with other men because I was bored or because Richard had hurt me in some way."

"And Richard went to bed with other women—"

"Because he was very macho about conquest. Very macho." She shook her head. "Except with me. We didn't make love for the last year of our marriage. He couldn't. He tried a few times but he couldn't quite do it. Then he very gallantly told me that he was just fine when he was with other women—just so I'd know that he was a real he-man. So don't get sanctimonious about my marriage, Mr. Dwyer. All right?"

"I apologize."

She laughed. "Maybe to go along with your contrition you should try a corn dog."

"I don't think so."

"A drink, then?"

"At noon hour?"

"You're such a prig, Mr. Dwyer. Lots of people have drinks at noon."

"Not people I know."

"Oh, yes, Dwyer the monk. It seems to me that if I could survive a corn dog, you could survive a drink."

"Well . . ."

"God, Mr. Dwyer, I'm not going to steal your cherry or anything. I'd like a drink."

So we went and had ourselves a drink.

5

"So do you like arresting shoplifters?"

"Not particularly."

"I wondered. I wouldn't like it either."

"Really?"

"Believe it or not, Mr. Dwyer, sad stories get to me. And I'll bet they're full of sad stories. Shoplifters, I mean."

"Fortunately for my delicate sensibilities, most of the people I bust are professionals. Very few people shoplift to get the essentials. Busting professionals doesn't bother me at all."

She raised her vodka gimlet and took a tidy sip. We were in a small shopping-mall bar, the sort where middle-class housewives and insurance salesmen come blinking in out of the daylight to be lost in the beery darkness. The only constant light is the rotating Bud clock suspended by a fancy gold chain from the ceiling. The jukebox runs to Engelbert Humperdinck. People kept coming in from outside, stamping snow off their feet.

"You must be very versatile."

"Why's that?" I asked, sipping my shell of Hamm's.

"Because the other day you were at the restaurant checking our security system and today you're arresting shoplifters."

"Which is what I usually do. Shoplifters. I was out at the restaurant the other day because the boss is on vacation in Bermuda until after the first of the year. Because I'm the only guy on staff who used to be a real cop, I cover a lot of bases for him."

She lighted a hundred-millimeter cigarette and inhaled deeply. You could almost hear the cancer cells applauding. "We never did get around to discussing it, my husband and I."

"Discussing what?"

"What you found."

"I didn't find anything."

"Nothing?"

She seemed quite surprised and that made me curious.

"What did you think I'd find, Mrs. Coburn?"

"Deirdre sounds so much better tripping off the tongue than Mrs. Coburn. I sound like a cleaning woman. 'Oh, Mrs. Coburn, and don't forget to take out the garbage, will you, dear?' "

"I thought we weren't going to irritate each other anymore. At least not on purpose."

"Did that irritate you?"

"Kind of, yeah. I had an aunt who was a cleaning woman."

"Aren't we the sensitive one, though."

I said, "What did you think I was going to find?"

"In the alley?"

"Yes."

"I wasn't sure."

"Who killed your husband?"

"My, you're really going to press me, aren't you?"

"You have some idea of who killed your husband. Otherwise you wouldn't have gone to all the trouble of looking me up."

"The police think it's Earle. Poor Earle."

"But you don't think so."

She smiled emptily at me. "No, I suppose I don't."

"So who killed him, Mrs. Coburn?"

"Now you're trying to irritate me, aren't you?" She tapped a long, perfect red nail on the edge of her glass. On the jukebox Nat "King" Cole started singing "The Christmas Song." I got sentimental but I wasn't sure about what. Maybe just his great voice.

She looked up at me. "I think it was that bitch Jackie."

"I don't know who she is."

"She was behind the bar when you were there the other day."

"Oh. Right. Her." I remembered the gorgeous brunette. "Why would she kill him?"

"She bought into the restaurant several weeks ago—her father had died and left her some money—and they hadn't been getting along very well, she and Richard. They disagreed on a lot of management practices."

"You'd better think over what you're saying. You're making a very serious charge."

"She did it." She sighed and stared into her drink

made silver in the backlight of the jukebox. "I'll pay you your normal rate."

"You want me to prove that Jackie killed him?"

"Yes."

"What if it turns out not to be Jackie?"

She raised her head and smiled. "Then you won't get a bonus." She paused. Smiled. There was a little warmth in this one. "I've already sent a check to your office. Two thousand dollars. That should get us started."

"I have a question for you."

"I may not have an answer."

"Your husband's partner seemed very upset the other day when he found out that I'd been looking around the building. I got the sense that he was hiding something—the same sense I got from your husband. Or maybe you're hiding something, Mrs. Coburn?"

She laughed and I realized then that she was slightly drunk. There was something melancholy about her being drunk in the middle of the afternoon in the company of a man who didn't like her. Something lonely that threatened to make her human to me. "I guess you'll just have to find out for yourself, Mr. Dwyer, won't you?"

I started to say something but then I decided to let "The Christmas Song" finish. I drank the rest of my shell.

"Did you ever read *The Great Gatsby*, Mr. Dwyer?"

"Several times."

"That was our problem. My husband and I."

"What was?"

"He came from a poor background and wanted to prove to the world that he was this wonderful, successful man. He really was Jay Gatsby. Unfortunately for both of us, I wasn't Daisy Buchanan."

The words had the feeling of a set piece, something she'd many times told lovers in many bars to assuage her guilt over adultery.

The front door opened and a big fat Santa Claus came in. He sat at a stool directly across from us and took off his hat and his fake white hair and his fake white beard. He was bald. He stuck a cheap cigar in his mouth and lighted it.

The bartender asked him, "How's it going today, Santa?"

Santa laughed and said, "This is one of them days when I feel sorry for child molesters. Gimme a double, Sammy, quick, okay?"

She said, "I wonder what I'll do Christmas. You know, I hadn't even thought of that till right now. Both my parents are dead."

She sounded drunk and sorry for herself, a state I was not unfamiliar with, and if I didn't quite like her a lot at least now I liked her a little.

"You're not so bad," I said.

"Do you mean that?" she said.

"C'mon," I said, "I'll walk you to your car."

6

After work I went home, showered quickly, put on my good blue suit, a white shirt with a gold tie bar, a deep red Wembley tie that had been my father's and was now back in style again, and my good black oxfords. In the bathroom mirror, I looked closely at my hair and decided it wasn't yet time for Grecian Formula, which my agent had lately been suggesting.

The Avanti blazed in the dark December night. There had to be two million dollars worth of cars in the parking lot. In the yellow overhead lights, snow blew furiously on the tundra of the macadam. The kid who parked my car was buried inside his parka. His eyebrows and mustache were white, snow frozen to them. He did not look happy to see the driver of a five-year-old Toyota. I could see him calculating his tip. He probably thought I'd leave him twenty-five cents.

The lobby was packed with women in minks and men in tuxedos, even a few double-breasted ones of the sort favored by Adolphe Menjou in gangster pictures. A maitre d' in a double-breasted tux himself looked slightly frazzled with all the business. He dispatched waiters like a German general sending soldiers into a battle against overwhelming odds.

It was hard to believe this was the same place I'd been in before, the place of piled chairs and muddy tracks across the dance floor. Night, and indirect lighting, changed everything. The art deco motif, all glass and chrome, lent the place a lively decadence. It looked like the sort of place where William Powell would have picked up Jean Harlow and that was fine by me. On the dance floor three dozen snotty night people tried to catch glimpses of themselves in the wall-length mirrors, and at the dinner tables any number of fat men were sampling the vintage while waiters stood by anxiously.

I told the maitre d' a lie, saying that I was to meet Mrs. Coburn in the bar. He looked as if he didn't quite believe me but was afraid to challenge me nonetheless.

I pushed my way into place at the bar just as the ten-piece orchestra went into "Love Walked In." The average age of the band members had to be mid-twenties but they had a sure and loving feel for the music they were playing.

I'd had two scotches and water when I saw him. Or rather when he saw me. I was under the impression he'd been staring at me for some time. Tom Anton, one of Richard Coburn's partners.

He wore, of course, a tuxedo and his sleeked-down hair still made him look like a road company Dracula and his face was still too pretty by half and his glossy dark eyes still cocaine dead.

But what was most interesting was the woman on his arm. Or girl, really. Tall, slender, got up in a simple white gown, her face regal but without even a glimmer of arrogance, she was dreamy in her youth and innocence, a princess in a corny 1950s movie about a coed who discovers she's really an heiress. She did not look at all dismayed about dating somebody Anton's age.

Everybody leaned eagerly forward to touch her and say hello, lending a definite aura of celebrity to the simple act of her walking down the length of the bar. Old men grinned and young men lusted. We're so accustomed to the hot and oversold sexuality of television that we forget how devastating grace and subtlety can be.

And how Anton enjoyed being at the center of it, even if it meant basking in her reflected glory. From a gold case, he took a cigarette without a filter. He had scarcely put it to his mouth when a smiling woman of fleshy charm brought from nowhere a tiny gold cigarette lighter and flamed him up. He smiled back at her. They were like two vampires sharing a private joke.

He turned his attention abruptly back to me. He eased from the girl's arm, whispering some sort of explanation or apology, and came over to me.

"My man at the front door tells me you're meeting Deirdre."

I nodded.

"You're a liar."

I forced a smile. "Are you this pleasant to all your customers?"

"Just the deadbeats."

"I do seem to be about the only guy here to-night not in a tuxedo."

"That's not the only thing you lack, Dwyer, believe me." He dragged deeply on the cigarette the woman had lighted for him. "I'd appreciate it if you'd leave."

"Mrs. Coburn hired me to find out who killed her husband."

"I know who killed her husband. Earle Tomkins."

"She doesn't seem to believe that."

"She's a very emotional woman."

"As long as you don't say sentimental."

"Richard wasn't easy to get along with, believe me. Deirdre may not be a saint but Richard was even less so."

"You don't look like much of a saint, either."

"Do you really think I give a damn what you think of me?" I nodded to the girl, whose crowd of admirers was now three deep. "She's a little young for you, don't you think, Anton?"

He smiled. Sneered, actually. "What an ass you are, Dwyer. Mignon is my daughter. She's sixteen." He shook his glossy head. "Now finish your drink and get the hell out of here."

With that, he turned back to the excitement behind him, the shy, elegant girl who was making all the men a little crazy.

"You walked right into that one," a voice said to my right. "Never give Tom an advantage like that."

At first, I didn't recognize her. When I'd seen her before she'd been dressed sensibly for work.

Tonight her dark hair was upswept into something so fancy I wasn't sure it had a name, and her gown was dark blue and wonderfully cut so as to reveal cleavage. She was still fifteen pounds overweight and it was lovely.

"Do you remember me?" she said.

"Now I do. Jackie."

"Right." She made a big production out of saying the word, dragging out the single vowel, and hinting that I'd probably just won some sort of prize or something. She was the senior girl you always had a crush on when you were a sophomore and not quite sure how to handle yourself. "Oh. Listen."

I wasn't sure what I was listening to. Or for.

" 'Laura.' The band."

"Ah," I said. "Right."

"I love that song."

"Actually, so do I."

She held white arms out to me. "Why don't we dance?"

"You'd dance in public with the only guy not in a tuxedo?"

She laughed. She had a slow, curiously weary laugh that made me like her. "I'd love to dance with the only guy not here in a tuxedo. I'm the only woman here not wearing real diamonds."

"Well, if you put it that way," I said, and we went out to the dance floor.

In seventh grade the nuns taught us how to do what they called the box step. You would stand embarrassed while a Sister of Mercy took you in tow around the gymnasium floor, showing you the art and etiquette of slow dancing, which mainly consisted of being a "gentleman and not a roughneck, Jack" and making sure you kept a ruler's worth of space between your chest and your partner's.

So tonight, on the dance floor with Jackie, I put the old box step into action.

"Ow," she said.

"Pardon?" I said. The orchestra was loud and I hadn't heard exactly.

"I said 'Ow.' "

" 'Ow'?"

" 'Ow.' You stepped on my foot. Twice, in fact."

"I'm sorry." And I was. And I felt embarrassed. I said, "I'm Fred Astaire's illegitimate son."

"Too bad you didn't get any of his talent."

I laughed. "Or his money."

She was short enough to put her head against my shoulder. Her hair smelled wonderful. Her fleshiness was warm and abundant and erotic in my arms. She took her head from my chest and looked up at me and said, "Why don't we just kind of hold each other and move around? That box step can be hell on a woman's instep. Who taught you anyway, your mother?"

"Sister Mary Rosalinda."

"Oh. Nuns. That explains it."

With that enigmatic remark, she placed her head against my shoulder and we did what she suggested, just held each other and moved around on the floor. It was a long number and during it I thought of a lot of things, everything from how I'd have to get a tuxedo someday to what I was going to get the kids for Christmas to how good it would be to see Donna again. I even thought of Richard Coburn and how his ego had dominated this place. I kept thinking of him as Jay Gatsby, the poor boy trying so uselessly to be something he was not and never could be, destroyed ultimately not by the mendacity of others but by his own self-indulgent naïveté.

"Are you hungry?"

"Sure," I said.

"They have great food here."

"I'm ready."

She made a yummy expression with her wide, tasty mouth. "So am I."

They had great goulash. I ate two bowls. Both times I cleaned my bowl out with my bread. Real truck driver stuff right here in the middle of all these society cokeheads.

"How're your feet?" I said.

"The nuns turned out some great football players, didn't they?"

"Wait till you see me dance fast."

"Is that a threat?"

She had a cigarette. She smoked as if she genuinely savored the taste. Apparently in café society, they had yet to hear of the surgeon general's anxiety.

Three stiff scotches and water had brought me some peace. I looked out over the restaurant, at the diners in their finery eating so politely, and for once I didn't dislike them, decided indeed that I was at least as much a snob about rich people as rich people were about working people. From my years as a policeman, I'd learned that malice and evil come in all sizes, shapes, colors, and social levels. It's tidy to divide the world into the evil rich and the noble poor but it doesn't work that way. I'd arrested a foundry worker who when sober and sane had beaten his wife to death because he didn't like the way she'd ironed his good white shirt for mass the next morning. As far as I know, he'd never expressed the slightest remorse during the trial, and went to the slammer still calling her a bitch. And I knew personally of a rich man who spent three Saturdays a month working at a soup kitchen.

I wasn't sure when the commotion started or even what it was all about.

"Oh, God," Jackie said.

I looked up from my drink and my thoughts. Somewhere near the lobby area, in the midst of a crowd, a scuffle or brawl of some kind was going on.

"Maybe I'd better see what's going on," she said. She sounded very proprietary. It made sense. She'd bought into the restaurant.

The orchestra continued to play, and play well, but you could see that everybody in the place was attuned to the problems at the front door.

At first, all I could see was three bulky men in

tuxedos going around in a furious black circle, sort of like the Tasmanian Devil in *Loony Tunes*. Somewhere in the center of the circle was a gray form they were trying to wrestle out the door. The men in tuxedos were cursing and shouting. The gray form was saying something keening and incomprehensible.

The onlookers looked both excited and horrified, women clutching men, men trying to look brave about it all. But it was sordid and frightening as all violence is sordid and frightening—the worst aspect of the human animal—and merely witnessing it you are diminished.

Finally, they pressed him to the wall, his arms spread crucifixion-fashion, and I got my first look at his madness and sorrow.

He was perhaps fifty, emaciated inside the filthy rags that fell from his sharp frail bones, all gaunt cheekbones and chin and ominous messianic gaze. He was one of the urban zombies, the poor and homeless there are so many of these days, the people we in equal parts so pity and despise.

One of the men hit him hard in the stomach and he doubled over and cried out.

In two steps I had the tuxedo man in a hammerlock and slammed him hard enough against the frame of a door to break his nose. For good measure I gave him a sharp kidney punch. Then I turned him around and slapped him once hard across the mouth. The fight went fast from him.

Jackie grabbed my arm. "Jesus Christ, Dwyer, calm down." So I calmed down. It came in stages.

I just stood there letting my heart and lungs find their natural levels. People stared at me. I felt embarrassed, a big stupid animal who hated violence so much that it made him violent. I suppose that didn't make any less sense than anything else in a world that makes no sense at all.

One of the tuxedo guys came up to Jackie. "Who is this asshole?" he said, jabbing a big thumb in my direction.

"A friend of mine," she said. Then she nodded to the doorway through which the homeless man had vanished. "There was no reason for Ken to hit him."

"He just got carried away."

"Well," she said. "That's what happened to Dwyer here. He just got carried away." She said it with a certain humor that the man refused to acknowledge.

He scowled at me and went over to where Ken was feeling his nose, blood having bloomed in his nostrils like tiny red flowers. Ken looked back at me and glowered and then the three men walked away.

"You need a drink," Jackie said.

"Two at least," I said.

By now people had lost interest. The band played "Tangerine." I let the strains of it bring me at least momentary peace as I sat back down at our table and Jackie obligingly ordered me a double.

"Why three bouncers?"

"For problems just like tonight. It's just how the city's laid out. Two blocks from the best section of restaurants is one of the worst areas for homeless people. They drift up to the front door and badger our customers. Occasionally they even get violent. That's why we have the bouncers."

I recalled the man in a Roman collar in the alley. The sad, crazed voice reciting Bible passages by rote. A short-sleeved shirt in the subzero temperature. In this city, as elsewhere, they were everywhere, bad and tawdry enough in daylight, but seeming to double in numbers and desperation at night. There was no money left for the homeless, and there were too many of them.

"I lost it a little there," I said, feeling the remorse that usually follows my violence. "I'm sorry."

She smiled into the candle glow. Each table was a tiny island tossing frail light against the crushing shadow. "What a perfect Catholic you are. Guilty guilty guilty."

"I take it you don't much like Catholics?"

"I distrust any religion whose leader is a man who wears a long white dress."

I finished my drink. The bouncers, including Ken, came to the small balcony on the west wall and stared down at the clientele. When their eyes settled on me, their faces grew tight and grim.

"He shouldn't have hit him," I said.

"Now you're going to rationalize."

"I overreacted but so did he."

"What children men are. All of you."

"Including Richard Coburn?"

"I knew we'd get to that."

"It's a fair subject."

She made a small, inscrutable gesture in the direction of the stiff-backed waiter. He nodded and began moving faster toward the bar.

"The word around the restaurant is that I killed him because we disagreed on how to run this place. Apparently I'm not only greedy but very important."

The waiter came. Given his obvious distaste when he was forced to serve me my drink, I assumed he was a good friend of Ken's.

I drank the scotch and water faster than I should have. I wasn't quite sure why. Maybe it was prolonged exposure to tuxedos. I am told that they can make certain types of people crazy after a certain amount of time. Maybe I'm one of those people.

"You don't look happy," she said.

"Am I supposed to look happy?"

"For what it's worth, I really do—did love him."

I watched her there in the soft candle glow. Just watched. And waited for her to speak again.

"He was a big, violent child who was almost psychotic about getting his own way. He had very specific goals and they mostly had to do with money and power and he didn't let anything stop him from reaching those goals." Instead of sounding critical about all these shortcomings, her voice was melancholy, even husky with loss. She smiled at the cool golden epicenter of the candle there beneath the red glass casing. "He was a wonderful lover." She glanced up. "I'm sure Deirdre told you he was impotent."

I didn't quite know how to answer that.

"Well, he was. With her." Her gaze fell again to the candle. "She's a real castrater. Always reminding him of his background, always telling him what a failure he was. She had a very public affair with Tom just to hurt him. This was right after he started having trouble in bed."

"With Tom Anton? His partner?"

"Ducky, eh? As she would say."

"So Coburn knew about it?"

"As I said, everybody knew about it. It only made Richard's sexual problems worse. That's why he turned to me. At least initially. Because I was nonthreatening. We didn't make love for the first five months. He was afraid to and I didn't want to push him. But the first night we tried, he succeeded. And he was wonderful. He really was."

She paused and said, "You're really getting potzed."

I stared down at my drink. Apparently I wanted to levitate it. I felt dizzy. "Jesus, but I'd like to go stand outside in the cold and snow for a while."

"Why don't you? I'll bring my car around."

"Are we going someplace?"

"You mean you haven't figured it out yet?"

"I guess not."

"I'm going to have you come over to my apartment for a dancing lesson."

I grinned. I felt fifteen. A slow, stupid, graceless fifteen. "You've never been hustled before, Dwyer?"

"Not that often."

"You look like a big dumb kid."

"Thanks."

"That was supposed to be endearing, you oaf."

"You sure you didn't put anything in my drink?"

She smiled: "Nothing permanently damaging."

Snowplows with the electric yellow eyes of insects came up the center of the wide avenue, gauzy behind blowing snow. I thought of this boulevard in my boyhood days, when an interurban car had run down the middle of the wide brick street. A bell always clanged pedestrians out of the way and the people aboard looked happy about being there. I used to take quarters from my paper route and ride the interurban all over the city, even out to the rolling hills west of the city limits.

Now freezing wind whipped silty snow in my face, sobering me. The cold made me feel alive again.

Limousines and Lincolns, sports cars and cars wanting badly to be sports cars, appeared and disappeared, disgorging passengers and picking them up. Even given the temperature and the wind and the snow, people were festive, smiling white privileged smiles at the tall black liveried doorman who had no smile at all.

And I knew I couldn't do it, be unfaithful. Donna and I had drifted apart lately, for reasons we either failed to understand or didn't wish to understand, but warm arms in the night would mean cold guilt in the morning. Donna was the only woman I'd ever been faithful to, and glum as I was about us, I didn't want to change that now.

I kept watching for a car—a silver Subaru she'd said—but none came.

Finally, a gorgeous woman bundled inside real mink trundled up and nudged me. Jackie looked up and smiled. "Feeling better?"

"Uh-huh."

"Sober?"

"Yup."

"Good." She grinned her wan grin again. "Because I'm having second thoughts."

"So am I."

"I really did love him." There in the spilled light of the restaurant, light the color of gold touching filthy city snow, she began to cry.

She leaned into me all perfume and alcohol vapors and kissed me wetly on the cheek. "You're really involved with somebody, aren't you?"

"Uh-huh."

"I admire you. Most men would have just come up to my apartment."

"Don't admire me too quickly. You don't know anything about me."

She huddled into her mink. "Are you walking to the parking lot?"

"Thought I would."

She offered me her arm. "It's slippery and a lady needs an escort."

We walked ten yards into the darkness—it was like being banished from Eden, the rich warm restaurant light receding, receding—and in the gloom I began seeing them, the ragged gray forms of the homeless staring at us, filthy faces and mad eyes.

"Oh, God," whispered Jackie, shuddering and holding me closer. "They scare me." Then, "I know that's superficial and I should be more sympathetic but they scare me."

Liberal guilt. I suffered from it, too. Despite all the public pronouncements to the contrary, there were probably some very sound reasons to fear certain homeless people. Many of them suffered terrible fits of depression and rage and disorientation—the gamut of mental illness—and consequently could become dangerous on occasion. Much as I felt sorry for them, I wasn't planning on taking any of them home with me for a meal.

The parking lot was vast and snowbound. Two black youths in parkas ran around getting cars and wheeling them around to the front of the restaurant. We were being midwestern and getting our own.

We found her car first. She got in, fired it up. Meanwhile, I took her scraper and cleared off her front and back windows. By now the cold was numbing. I didn't know how the homeless nearby stood it, or why they weren't in shelters.

When I finished with the scraper, I tossed it on the backseat of her Subaru. As I leaned over, she kissed me gently on the mouth. It was a wonderful kiss and I really appreciated it.

"I think we could have had a really nice time," she said. She was not in any way coy or teasing.

Indeed there was regret in her voice now. "Nice warm bodies on a cold lonely night."

"But we had to go and be mature about it all," I said.

She dropped the Subaru in gear. "Yes," she said. "Isn't it the shits?"

I stood back to let her fishtail her way out of the parking lot. I went down two rows and got the scraper off the seat of my Toyota and did the front and back windows and dropped into the driver's seat and closed the door and turned on the ignition and got some rock on the radio and went home, hoping all the time there would be a message from Donna waiting.

But no rod light on the answering machine shone in the darkness of my apartment and I sat by the frost-rimmed window for a long time watching the snowflakes fall past the streetlight on the corner and wondering what she was doing now and if she was alone and if she was thinking of me. Perhaps she wasn't alone and was thinking of me anyway. We're like that sometimes, we humans.

8

Once Earle Tomkins had formally been charged with murder, they'd moved him over from city lockup to county jail, which is a place at Christmastime that could turn Mother Teresa to despair.

I suppose it's all the little kids the Sheriff lets visit in the days before Christmas. A lot of them haven't seen their daddies for a while and so they go a little crazy there in the big gray room where you visit prisoners while chunky guards in starchy blue uniforms walk around in leather-creaking shoes and leather-creaking holsters bearing big silver Magnums. Most of the daddies run to the sort of forlorn criminals who still fill most of our prisons—the car thieves, the dealers in hot merchandise, the generally harmless breaking-and-entering types, the tavern brawlers who got unlucky and had an opponent slip and give himself a concussion. When you talk to them you realize that they have one thing in common—they're not very smart. They'll do ninety days to a year for their various offenses and then they'll get out and things will go all right for a few months and then they'll be back again, not any smarter at all. But there's a new type in there with them now, the dope people, and while they may not be any smarter, they're meaner. There was a time, even back when I was a cop and before

Donna started working me over with her liberal-
ism, when I thought that maybe the death penalty
should be put away after all, that it served no real
purpose. But the Eighties and street drugs brought
me back around again. Either we kill them or they'll
kill us.

Of course, all the little kids crying and clinging
to their daddies now knew nothing of this that
snowy gray morning as I waited for sight of Earle
Tomkins. The little kids always asked the same
thing, over and over—why can't you come home,
Daddy, why can't you come home? —and if you're
an onlooker, you have to look away or the eyes and
voices of the little ones will crush you.

Tomkins turned out to be exactly who I thought
he might, the young man Coburn had yelled at for
tracking mud across the dance floor. Unlike ninety-
nine percent of the other prisoners, Tomkins looked
as if he didn't belong here. Even in his red prisoner jumpsuit, he kept an air of dignity and purpose and intelligence. The guard led him over to
the table in the far corner where I sat idly leafing
through an issue of *Time* magazine so old Jimmy
Carter was on the cover.

He sat down and stared at me.

"Do you remember me, Earle?"

"Sort of."

"I was at the restaurant a few days ago, sitting
with Richard Coburn."

"That's right," he said, remembering. Then he
said, in a quiet voice, "I didn't kill him."

I put my hand out. He took it and we shook.

When I brought my hand back, I said, "I'm a private investigator."

"You are?"

"Yes."

He had a cleanshaven face and good features by which, I suppose, I meant white features. Like it or not, we all use our own respective race as the measure of animal attractiveness.

"Did you work full-time at the Avanti?"

"No, I'm in junior college. I'm going to transfer to the university next year as soon as I finish this year." He looked flustered and embarrassed. "I mean, I was until all this came up." For the first time, I heard panic and bitterness in his voice. "I really didn't kill him."

"You were mad at him?"

He smiled. "Everybody was mad at him. All the time. I hope he wasn't a friend of yours—I mean, the man was a prick. No two ways about it."

"So I gather."

"Then he wasn't a friend of yours?"

"Nope. I was working for him the same as you."

Behind us, there was some hassle as a prisoner and his wife got into a shouting match. You see that a lot. Prisoners get to thinking they're the isolated ones, locked up here in this three-story fortress with bars on the windows. But their faithful wives, home with three scruffy kids and not enough money to make the rent or decent meals, are every bit as isolated. And so once in a while they come up here in their poor faded dresses with their poor faded children and their poor faded hopes and they can't take it anymore, they were girls just a few years ago and now somehow they're bitter old women even if by the calendar they're only twenty-two or -three, and if their husbands have even an inkling of this, they're too macho or too plain stupid to ever let on. So the women yell sometimes; it's all they have left to them.

When I turned back to Earle Tomkins, he said, suspicious now, "How come you're here?"

"I want to find out who murdered Coburn."

"You don't think I did?" Hope shone in his eyes. I had to dash it.

"Maybe you did, maybe you didn't. That's what I want to find out."

"But you haven't ruled out that I'm innocent?"

I decided to give the kid some hope back. "I'd say there's at least a fifty-fifty chance you are innocent."

He grinned and I thought of my own son. "No shit, Mr. Dwyer, you really believe that? That I could he innocent?"

"I really believe that."

"Would you do me a favor?"

"If I can."

"Call my mom and tell her that, would you? I'm the only son still at home, and my dad's dead, and she's alone and this really devastated her."

"Give me the number."

He did and I wrote it down in my open note-book, which lay on the table before me.

I said, "According to the police reports I saw earlier this morning, you were seen running away from Coburn's car in the parking lot. A few seconds later several restaurant employees found Coburn dying."

"Somebody was wearing my jacket and stocking cap."

"Three of the employees made a positive identification."

"Think about it, Mr. Dwyer."

"You could always call me Jack. 'Mr.' always makes me feel like the kind of guy who forecloses mortgages on old ladies."

He smiled. "Okay, Jack. But think about it. You see somebody in a bright red windbreaker with the collar turned all the way up and dark blue stocking cap pulled down over the face. That's all you really see—so it's pretty easy to imagine that it's me inside. But it could have been anybody, especially since it was night. Man or woman. Anybody."

"How would somebody get your windbreaker?"

"When I came up from the basement, where I usually stack liquor in the early evening, it was gone."

"I thought you worked in the morning."

"Three days a week, I work split shifts." He paused. "You write everything down?"

"Just about. You can never tell when a piece of information will come in handy. That's a holdover from my days on the force, I guess."

"You were a cop?"

I looked at him. "Cops aren't in danger of being your favorite people, eh?"

"I wouldn't go that far."

"Well, believe it or not, most cops are decent guys." I'd resented his tone more than I'd realized.

"Not in my neighborhood."

I shrugged. "You know what, Earle? Maybe we better not talk about cops."

He shook his head, turning back grimly to his own problem. "I didn't kill him."

"I hope you're telling the truth, Earle." I smiled. "If you are, and we can prove it, your mother's going to have a damn nice Christmas."

"I think it was that Daily woman."

"What Daily woman?"

"The woman who runs the homeless shelter—you know, St. Mark's—a few blocks from the restaurant."

"Why would she kill him?"

"I don't know why, Jack, but I sure know they had a lot of arguments."

"How do you know that?" I was scribbling in my notebook again.

"I told you I stack liquor at night?"

"Right?"

"Well, right over the storage area was where Coburn had his office. Anton's office is further down the hall. Anyway, sometimes they'd get to arguing so loud I couldn't help but hear. They were right above me."

"And you don't know what they were arguing about?"

"Not exactly. Something about the shelter. But I'm not sure what."

"How many times did you hear them arguing?"

"Uh, I don't know. Maybe a dozen or so."

"Over how long a span of time?"

He thought it over. "Couple months, maybe."

"When was the last time they argued?"

"Week or so before he was killed."

"You're positive?"

"Positive."

"And you're also sure it was this Daily woman?"

"Absolutely. After I heard them arguing a couple of times, I got curious about who it was so I went upstairs and kind of hung out near his office so I could get a look at her. It was her, all right."

"And you don't have any idea why a woman from the homeless shelter would be arguing with a man like Coburn?"

"Not unless it had something to do with those old dudes who're always bothering our customers."

"A lot of problems?"

"A lot."

"Did Coburn ever say anything to you about the homeless who stayed around the restaurant entrance?"

"He said something to everybody. He used to get so pissed his face would get red."

"Maybe that's what Coburn and Daily were arguing about." I wanted him to give me his initial, visceral impression of what had been going on.

But apparently he was finished. "Maybe."

I closed my notebook. "Would your mother be at home now?"

"Not till tonight. She wraps packages down at Barrengers." Barrengers was a department store.

I stood up and shook his hand again. "I'll call her tonight, Earle."

"I really appreciate this, Jack."

Seeing me on my feet, the guard came over.

"I sure hope you find something out, Jack," Earle said to me as I was leaving. "I sure hope you do."

9

On the way over to the homeless shelter, the sun came out yellow against a blue sky. Despite the fifteen-below temperature, it was like a preview of spring and along the old yet well-kept houses of Third Avenue, some of which still had livery stables in their backyards, you could see people smiling a little more often than they did on gray days. Tots in bulky snowsuits and pretty young mothers in the latest variations on greatcoats and stocking caps ambled along the sidewalk, glimpsing themselves in the trendy windows of the boutiques.

I had to pass the Avanti to reach St. Mark's. In the restaurant parking lot, I saw Tom Anton get out of a new green XKE. Without quite knowing why, I pulled my Toyota into the slick lot and parked behind him.

By the time I climbed out of my car, he had disappeared into a side door. He hadn't seen me.

I was about to turn back when I saw Anton's daughter, Mignon, suddenly sit up in the seat. She had been bent over, not as if hiding, but occupied with something on the floor.

I went over to her and knocked on the window.

"Hello, Mr. Dwyer."

"I'm impressed. We weren't even introduced the other night."

"Oh, but I remember my father telling me about you."

I laughed. "I can imagine how that went."

She smiled softly. In the morning light, she looked both younger and older than her years, the bones of her face more delicate, the dark eyes more grave. In her blue ski jacket and startling white blouse, her dark hair pulled back into a ponytail, she was still out of Edgar Allan Poe via the country club. "I don't always agree with my father."

"You don't, eh?"

"No. He told me you were a very angry man and I should avoid you."

"And what did you say?"

"I said you didn't look angry to me. Just kind of sad."

"I see."

Her eyes scanned my face. "I embarrassed you, didn't I?"

Here I'd been standing in a snow-white parking lot letting the yellow sun warm me and feeling like a lazy uncomplicated animal, and then she went and made it midnight and very adult.

"I'm sorry I embarrassed you. You were really blushing."

"That's all right. I just didn't expect to talk about sadness on such a beautiful morning."

"I'm sad, too, Mr. Dwyer. When I saw you the other night, I sensed right away that you and I were very much alike."

"Now why would a beautiful young girl like yourself be sad?"

She shook her head. It was one of those gestures that made her look young—ponytail flying—as others made her look old. I tried not to notice the sensual fullness of her mouth. Instead of answering me seriously, however, she kidded me. "Well, for one thing, even beautiful young girls have trouble getting their boots on."

"Boots?" She opened the door. The XKE had a lovely smell of new and genuine car leather.

She had one mid-calf cowboy boot on. The mate sat on the floor. "I can't seem to get it on. It's unusually tough but not this tough. That's why I just wore some Capezios this morning when we left the house. I thought I'd pull this on while I was waiting for Tom."

"Tom?"

"I'm very sophisticated, Mr. Dwyer. I call my father Tom. He actually seems to like that. The other girls envy me. Their fathers are very old-fashioned." She was a kid again, nattering. Then, "Would you help me?"

"If I can."

"If I put my leg out the door, will you try and tug the boot on?"

"Actually, I used to moonlight selling shoes back when I just got out of police school."

"Tom said you used to be a policeman."

"Tom seems to have taken an interest in me."

For the first time, I sensed evasion in her. "It's

just Richard's—death. Tom's usually very nice about things. But Richard's death upset him." She kept her eyes on the side door in the brick wall of the restaurant, as if her father might come charging out of there at any moment. "He couldn't sleep last night."

"Oh?"

"But then, I couldn't either. We were both thinking about Richard. Richard always got his way; he's certainly not somebody you could forget easily." I tried to understand her tone. There was a curious deadness in it. She was relating emotions, not feeling them.

"What do you mean Richard always got his way?"

She shrugged. "With Tom. With his wife. With everybody, really." She thought a moment. "He—pushed. Everybody and everything."

"You didn't like him?"

"I—felt sorry for him sometimes."

"Is that anything close to liking him?"

She shrugged. "He was like us, I guess, Mr. Dwyer."

"Us?"

"You and I."

"Oh."

"He had his sorrow."

"I see."

"And so I couldn't hate him. It's pretty hard to hate anybody, when you really think about it."

Abruptly, she handed me the boot. It was Texas-

style and alligator and expensive. She pushed forth
her leg at the end of which was a wiggly little size-
six foot covered in a clean white sweat sock with a
bright red circle at the top.

"You think you can do it?"

"I'll try."

She giggled. "Cinderella."

I started to ease the boot on. She had the ankle
of a colt, so slender. I had the sense I could snap it.
I was careful, so careful.

"Your face is getting red," she said.

"Thanks for pointing that out."

"I wonder if the prince's face got red."

"The prince?"

"In Cinderella. When he was sliding the glass
slipper on."

"Ah."

So I pushed some more, and tugged, and I
thought of my shoe-selling job. Holding the sweaty
feet of others is not my idea of a fun profession.
(No, ma'm, I don't have a shoe in your particular
size of gunboat but maybe I could squeeze you into
one of these boxes here.)

I said, "Did your father and Richard ever have
arguments?"

"Oh, sure. Richard had arguments with everyone."

"How about recently?"

"Did they have an argument recently, you
mean?"

"Yes."

Hesitation. "I thought you and I were going to be friends."

I looked up from where I was just about finished turning and twisting the boot into place. "Gee, I hope we still are."

"Then please don't try to make me incriminate Tom." She was older again; and angry. "Tom didn't kill Richard, if that's what you're getting at."

I stood up. The exertion had put a light sheen of sweat on my face. "I'm sorry if I hurt your feelings, Mignon."

"Tom may not be perfect but he's my father and I love him very much. My mother died of cancer when I was seven years old and I think, all things considered, that Tom has done a very good job raising me." She had fixed me with her lovely dark gaze. "I want you to believe me."

"About Tom?"

"Yes."

"That he didn't kill Richard?"

"Yes."

"All right."

She shook her head. "I only wish you meant that."

"I don't think Earle Tomkins killed him."

"Perhaps not."

"That would most likely leave the people closest to him."

"It could have been a stranger. A robbery."

"The police report says that more than two thousand dollars in bills was found in his wallet and that he was wearing a wristwatch valued at three thousand dollars. I'm afraid that doesn't support a robbery theory, Mignon."

"Well, it wasn't Tom."

"All right."

The door in the side of the building banged shut. Tom Anton walked toward us. For a few feet, before he saw me, he slid on the ice like a kid. The resemblance between father and daughter was strong—the almost glossy good looks, the Aspen ski tan, the sense of sorrow Mignon spoke of so freely, almost romantically.

When he looked up and saw me, he stopped as if he'd just realized he was walking into a trap of some sort. He even looked around, as if for places to run and hide.

Then he composed himself, put on his arrogant smile, gave his step a jauntiness, nudged up the collar of the ski jacket that matched Mignon's, and then came up the shining rut of ice toward us.

"I'd prefer you not talk to my daughter, Dwyer," he said. "I'd just as soon she not know people like you exist."

"Please, Tom," she said.

He stood in the sunlight glaring at me.

Mignon said, "He helped me get my boot on, Tom."

Anton did not look pleased that my infidel's hand had been laid anywhere on his daughter's body. He said, "I hope Deirdre is happy. It's not bad enough that poor Richard is murdered and that the restaurant suffers all the bad publicity—now she wants to keep everything going by having you pester all of us."

"She doesn't think Earle Tomkins killed him."

He laughed. "My God, Dwyer, are you that naive? Can't you see that you were hired just to bother us? She doesn't give a damn about Tomkins. Deirdre is a very spoiled woman who never got over the fact that she drove her husband into the arms of another woman. Deirdre wants anything she can't have."

"She seems to think Jackie killed Richard."

"That isn't why she hired you, Dwyer."

"No?"

"No. As I said, she hired you to bother all of us but we shut her out long ago. She's a very destructive woman." He looked around again; and once more I had the impression that he wanted to run and hide somewhere. "And she hired you to find out what Richard was so afraid of."

"I don't know what you're talking about."

"Neither do I, exactly. But she seems to think that something was going on here at the restaurant—something worth discovering. Something only Richard knew about. That's why she really hired you. To find out what Richard was hiding—and to have the pleasure of seeing you keep Jackie and me unhappy."

He had started, by the end, to speak to me in something like a civil tone. I returned the favor. "You really don't know what Richard was hiding?"

"No."

"How do you know he was hiding anything at all?"

"Because he took to locking his office. And questioning our chef mercilessly to the point where the man quit. In case you don't know anything about chefs—or the best ones anyway—they're not easy to come by."

"What was this chef's name?"

"Sal Umbretti."

"He's still in the city?"

He frowned. "Yes, he's now working for our chief competitor. Their business is up, I'm told, about twenty percent."

"What made him quit?"

"I'm not sure—except that one night a customer found something in his food and made a big stink about it. That's all I know. Umbretti was very upset." He shot his sleeve and consulted his wristwatch. "I have to go." Then he took out a pair of mirror sunglasses and slipped them on.

Through the windshield, Mignon stared at me. She looked lost.

Anton got in the car, slid behind the wheel. With his hundred-dollar haircut and his mirror sunglasses and his black leather driving gloves, he looked as if God had put him on this planet for no other reason than to sit behind the wheel of an XKE.

He slammed the door and put the car in gear. Mignon continued to stare at me.

Anton didn't say goodbye or even look in my direction. Somehow that didn't surprise me.

But as they pulled from the lot, Mignon glanced back once, just once. I thought of the way she called her father Tom. I didn't know why but that made me feel badly for both of them.

10

A man was on his hands and knees crawling around in the filthy sidewalk snow. He looked a week past shaving and smelled even longer past a bath. He wore a threadbare long Army coat and a Navy stocking cap. He made a vague grab at me as I approached the entrance to St. Mark's. I started to walk wide when another man appeared in the double doors, glanced nervously around, and then found the man he'd apparently been looking for right beneath his eyes. "Donald! Donald, now you stand up and get in here. Gwen's been looking for you for the past fifteen minutes. She was about ready to call the cops."

The man in the doorway wore the sort of faded good clothes you find in Goodwill—once expensive but now given dignity by their cleanliness and the fact that they clothed a poor man. The man had the sharp quick eye of a zealot. He was sober, cleanshaven, clear-eyed. He'd probably become an assistant to the woman who ran the shelter and he took his job with TV-minister seriousness.

"Now you get up here," he said again, sounding almost motherly as he bent over to help the drunkard to his feet. He was tall and angular and sour and in his next incarnation would probably be a Presbyterian minister.

He had no luck with the drunkard. Oh, he got him to his feet all right but then they started doing Laurel and Hardy, sliding around on the ice, a slippery ballet.

"Would you be so kind, sir, as to give me a hand here?" He was obviously restraining himself, wanting to call me a worthless sonofabitch for just standing there, but the responsibility of his job forbade such indulgence. "Please?" he said then, remembering the old please-and-thank-you of our youth.

I went over and got the drunk man under the arms. This close, he really smelled rancid. Sometime not too long ago he'd filled his pants. I held him tight and started pushing him, like this big sled, toward the entrance doors.

The drunkard had no qualms about calling me names. "Fuckin' bas'ard, lemme go!" And then tried to shrug me off. He had wild pitiful brown eyes covered now by a gauzy membrane that resembled cataracts. I walked him in lock step up to the doors, pushed him flailing up the three steps, and then shoved him inside the vast stone building that had once been a Catholic church. He was bringing back a lot of unpleasant memories of when I'd been a beat cop trying to push violent drunks into the backseats of patrol cars.

Inside what had once been the vestibule, the drunkard started back for the door. The other man slammed into him with a body block that would have done a pro football player proud. "Now, Donald, you just calm down. We're going to clean you up and get you sober." He looked at me and shook his head. He looked back at the drunkard. "My name is Ron as I already told you, but you probably don't remember that." He stared straight into the man's face. Given the man's bodily odors, Ron was a hell of a lot braver man than I would have been. "Now we're going down the corridor here to the showers and I don't want any trouble, all right?"

Even now, probably not too far from death from alcohol poisoning, the drunkard had some resources. He started pushing something that vaguely resembled a punch in Ron's direction and said, "Fuckin' bas'ard."

Ron looked at me and shook his head again. "Could I help you, sir?"

"I'd like to see the woman who runs the shelter."

"Gwen Daily?"

"If she's in charge."

"Could I tell her who's asking for her?" He sounded distrustful. Maybe they got assassins coming here a lot.

I started to give him my name but the drunkard took another swing. This time he ended up on the floor. Ron put his hands on his hips. The motherly tone was back. "I hope you're proud of yourself, Donald. I hope you're proud of yourself."

"Jack Dwyer's my name."

He raised his head from Donald and said, "And you're with?"

"American Security."

He seemed to chew on that awhile, apparently trying to figure out exactly what American Security might be.

"If you'll keep an eye on him, I'll go tell Gwen you're here."

I nodded and he left. He went through two very wide doors that had once led to the church interior but that now led to a short row of office doors on either side of a whitewashed narrow corridor. At the end of the corridor was another door and from beyond that you could hear the talk and the laughter and the coughing of men in the morning, men who'd drunk too long and smoked too much. It sounded like a ward in a veterans' hospital.

"Fuckin' bas'ard," Donald said again from his position in the center of the floor.

"You'll be all right. Just calm down."

"Sonofabitch," he said.

I was tired of him already.

Ron came back. "How's he doing?"

"Just great."

"No trouble?"

"We're the best of friends, Donald and I."

He frowned at my sarcasm. "He just kind of gets me down is all," I said.

He got wound tight again. "If we all thought like that, then nobody would take care of the poor and homeless now, would they?"

He had a point. "I shouldn't have said that. I'm sorry."

Ron sighed. "You're not any worse than others,

I suppose. You see somebody like Donald here and you can't quite convince yourself that he's a human being just like you. It's the only way you can deal with him—otherwise you'd have to face some very ugly facts about our society."

I didn't want to hear any more socialist messages this morning so I went over and bent down and got Donald to his feet. "Where do you want him?" I asked.

"I can do this. You don't have to."

"Catholic guilt."

"What?"

"Nothing."

I helped bring Donald down to the end of the corridor. Ron opened the door. Inside was the cavernous remains of the church. The gothic architecture of the exterior—with its huge spire soaring right up from the roof of the church—was continued in here. High ribbed vaulting and fine window tracery enveloping beautiful stained glass paintings of a solemn Jesus and a radiant Mary glowed in the sunlight. Everything that had once been on the floor—altar, pews, baptismal station—had been torn out and replaced by a gymnasium-like arrangement that resembled one of those shelters run by the Red Cross following a natural disaster—a flood or tornado. Cots and single beds lined the walls. Strung down the middle was an endless clothesline on which hung drying T-shirts and underwear and shirts and work pants. Maybe a hundred men milled around, some fully dressed, some just in long johns. I thought of Depression Oakies in the Dust Bowl. Radios battled—country-western, rock, even, unlikely as it seemed, FM playing Brahms. The air smelled of sweat, sleep, cigarette smoke, and gallons of Aqua Velva blue.

"Just leave him here," Ron said. He nodded back to the corridor. "Gwen's office is the middle one." He smiled. Now I saw why he didn't smile more often. The few teeth he had were black. "And thanks, Dwyer. God will bless you for your kindness."

His formality embarrassed me. He could have just left it at thanks. I nodded and left, taking a last look as I did. This was the final stop just before you pushed off to the final darkness. So many failed lives here. So little you could do for them really, just let them pace around in the cages of their sorrow.

Gwen Daily's office was painted yellow with orange flowers on it. The sort of hand-done stuff that smacked of giving a resident a paintbrush and saying, Be creative. I'm sure the guy had a great time doing it all.

The office furnishings weren't much better, the sort of chipped, smashed, and battered stuff you get at bankruptcy sales. Gwen Daily appeared to be about thirty. She had soft brown hair cut stylishly short and soft brown hazel eyes busy with some accountancy sheets on her desk. In her right hand, arched in the mannered but attractive way of a model, burned a filter-tip cigarette in direct violation of the NO SMOKING PLEASE sign on the wall. She had a cute little wrist and fingernails so badly bitten that you could see where they bled through the skin sometimes. She wore a plain white blouse with a necklace of outsize brown beads. If I hadn't already glimpsed her eyes, I probably would have mistaken her for a working single mother who didn't get enough sleep and probably hadn't shared a bed with a fellow in several long lonely months. But I had seen the eyes and they were the same sort of eyes prim Ron had shown me, a zealot's eyes, part grief, part rage. She looked up and said, "Yes?"

"Gwen?"

"Yes."

"I'm Dwyer."

"Dwyer?"

"Didn't Ron mention me?"

"Oh. Right. Dwyer. Sorry. I just got lost in some figures. Sit down if you'd like."

"Thanks."

"Like some coffee?"

"Please."

"I make it pretty strong."

"I like it pretty strong."

She got up and walked over to a metal bookcase packed with what appeared to be bound government reports and textbooks on, God forbid, sociology. Cops always figure sociologists should have bounties on their heads.

The seat I took was a green leatherette-covered armchair that made an embarrassing *whooshing* sound when I sat down. The whooshing made me want to apologize—one of those idiot social moments—but I figured that by now she was probably used to the sound the chair made. The right arm was taped with dirty-gray electrician's tape and the left one was covered with cigarette burns.

She poured two cups of coffee and brought them over. She wore a brown tweed skirt that touched just below her knees. She had very nice legs. The brown pumps surprised me a bit. They not only emphasized the clean lines of her calves but seemed a little dashing all on their own. Somehow she didn't seem the sort.

She served me coffee in a white ceramic mug with the name JIM painted on the side of it. The mug had two flowers more or less identical to the ones on the wall. Somebody had to stop this guy and soon.

She went back around behind her desk and sat down and said, "So exactly what is American Security, Mr. Dwyer?"

"It's a security agency that also does private investigative work and I'll pay you a dollar if you'll just call me Jack."

She had a quick warm girlish laugh. I liked her on the spot for it. "I wish all our dollars were that easy to raise here at St. Mark's."

"Tough, huh?"

"People hate poor people. They did in Christ's time and they're no different now."

"Why don't you hate poor people?"

"Because I am now and always have been a 'poor people' myself." She made cute little invisible quotation marks with her cute little bitten-up fingers. "My father was an alcoholic carpenter and my mother suffered all her short and painful life from rheumatoid arthritis." She stubbed her cigarette out in an otherwise clean ashtray. "I'm waiting for you to make some sarcastic remark about the no-smoking sign."

"Far be it from me."

"Everybody else comes in here and smokes. I figure I should get to, too. Though I'm trying to quit."

"Me too," I said.

"You've tried?"

"Several times. Haven't smoked for nearly two years now."

"Do you miss it?"

"Not more than thirty or forty times a day."

She laughed her quick warm laugh again. "Gosh, thanks for the encouragement."

"You don't get sick of them?"

"Of who?"

"Of poor people."

"Oh, sure. Half the time I hate them. I look at them and say, You lazy, shiftless bums, why don't you get your act together and clean yourself up and go out and get a job?"

"You say it to them?"

"Of course not. They hate themselves enough already. I say it to myself. Then I pray and ask for patience and wisdom."

"Do you ever get them?"

"Patience, maybe. Wisdom, not so far as I can tell."

"Do you ever think of quitting?"

"Constantly. But social work is about all I'm cut out for. I spent ten years in the welfare department as a caseworker but one day something happened and I just quit."

"Bad, huh?"

"Terrible." Her hazel eyes got weary. "We found that this one worker had been sloughing off pretty badly. There were clients he hadn't contacted or visited in months. He got canned—which is a considerable achievement in the welfare department, believe me—and so we divided up his list to visit. One afternoon I go up the stairs of this really filthy apartment building—four flights up—and I get to the door and I knock and the smell is so bad I can't believe it. Even through the closed door. I tried the knob and it was open. I went inside and it was horrible. Garbage and the leavings of drugs and dogs all over the place. I called out for somebody but nobody answered. Several of the windows had been smashed open. it was about as cold as it is today. I walked all over that place looking in closets and under couches and in the bathroom so I could make a report. And then under the bed I found her. This little four-month-old baby girl—that's how old they put her age at later—and at first I thought I was hallucinating. I was down on my knees staring under the bed where her mother or whoever had left her and I just couldn't believe it. That's where the odor was coming from. The little girl was dead and bloated and all discolored and you could see where a dog had eaten parts of her away. I had kind of a breakdown. I hated myself for doing it but I couldn't help it. I took the seven weeks of vacation I'd accumulated and I went on one of those cruises where you stay drunk all the time and flirt with every man in sight." She offered me a rueful smile. "I wouldn't have blamed God for being pretty p.o.'d at me, carrying on the way I did, I mean."

"You make God sound like a pretty mean person."

"Sometimes he should be. He should be very mean to the woman who left that child to die under that bed. And he should be very mean to me for not being tougher." She shrugged fragile shoulders. "Anyway, I never did go back. St. Mark's had an opening as an assistant, so I took it. I don't have to deal with children here. I can't take seeing children hurt or killed. That's where my courage and compassion end. I think very uncharitable thoughts about adults who hurt children."

"I used to be a cop. I used to think of killing some of the parents I met. Sneaking up at night and killing them in their sleep."

"It wouldn't have bothered you, killing somebody like that?"

"Not in my fantasies it didn't. Maybe reality would have been different." This was one of those moments—adrenaline flowing—when a cigarette would have been nice. "I got sick of seeing children beaten and sexually abused."

"You sound as bitter as I am."

"I probably am."

"And you do what exactly now, Jack?"

"Work on security matters."

"That's why I'm having a hard time guessing why you're here."

As soon as I told her why, her friendly tone would disappear. She would be tight and suspicious and she wouldn't like me at all and I wanted her to like me. I thought of Donna and how she hadn't called for the first three days of her convention and I wanted this woman to like me a great deal.

I said, "I'm told you knew a man named Richard Coburn."

"My God."

"'My God'?"

"You're here because of Richard?"

"Yes."

"People told you I used to go over to the restaurant and that we'd get into arguments, didn't they?"

"Yes."

"And being a good cop, you want to know what we argued *about* right?"

"Right."

"My God."

"What?"

She seemed genuinely flustered, her cheeks faintly red. "I just can't believe I'm being implicated in this."

"You're not being implicated in this."

"Then why are you here?"

"To find out what your arguments were about."

"Right."

"Why don't you have another cigarette and calm down?"

"Please don't say that."

"Say what?"

"'Calm down.' I hate it when people say that. It always sounds so patronizing."

"Well, I'm sorry, but you seem genuinely upset and I hate to see you that way is all."

"Oh, yes, I'm sure you're a very sensitive soul."

"You really think I had that coming?"

The blush again. She sat up straight. She put her shoulders back. "I'm sorry. You're right. You don't deserve that." She took sharp tiny breaths. She was composing herself. "I guess it had to come out eventually. I'm just so ashamed. It's so—stupid."

"What is?"

"What I did."

"What did you do?"

"Went out with him."

"With Coburn?"

"Yes."

For some reason I felt disappointed and betrayed. It was dumb to feel that way, but there it was. "For how long?"

"On and off for a month."

"I see."

"He was everything I was supposed to hate. But there was something appealing about him. At first, anyway. He was still married—technically, at least—and he had a girlfriend named Jackie. He needed a friend, he said. He wanted me to be that friend. That's when he was most appealing, when he needed—help. He was almost like a little boy. I suppose I have this strong maternal urge. Anyway, I'd gone to the Avanti for a drink one night and that's where I'd met him and somehow we ended up in a booth and we were both sort of drunk and he looked very handsome in a rough way and I was very lonely and so it just sort of started. Of course we both agreed that it would be nothing more than a platonic thing and of course it immediately became something else. He started taking me to this motel, the Wanderleigh. My God, it was like being in college again. I fell in love with him. I couldn't help it. It was stupid and hopeless and I was ashamed of myself." She stopped and put a fingernail in her mouth and bit it. At least for the moment, she seemed to have run out of words.

"How long did it go on?"

"In high school I fell in love with a football hero. I hate football and I hate heroes. It was sort of that way with Richard. I didn't respect what he did for his living, or his values, but I fell in love with him anyway."

I said, "So how long did it go on?"

"A little over a month."

"He cut it off?"

"Yes. But not for the reason you think."

"Oh?"

"He was convinced I knew something about some letters he was receiving."

"What sort of letters?"

"That was just it. He'd get very angry and paranoid but he wouldn't tell me anything. just that somebody from the shelter here was sending him letters."

"So you never saw the letters?"

"No."

"And he never told you their contents?"

"No. But he did start getting very abusive about homeless people. He started telling me that they were just bums who were too lazy to work. You know, the standard accusations. And his people started being very rough with them at their door. Pushing them away if they bothered the customers in any way. The homeless have rights, too."

I said, as gently as possible, "But they don't have the right to harass people. You may feel sorry for them and I may feel sorry for them but people going into dinner have the right to do that in peace, without being panhandled or insulted or threatened."

"And meanwhile the homeless starve."

"That's for government or places like yours to handle. It's not the responsibility of people going out to dinner or hurrying to work."

"You're a difficult man to read, Jack. Just when I think I've got you figured out, you surprise me."

"So what were your arguments about?"

She started gnawing on a hangnail. "Ostensibly

about the way he was treating the homeless who'd wander by his place. One night it got very had. One of the men who lived here on and off—he'd fall off the wagon for a couple of weeks at a time and then wander back here—was named Smiley. I was never sure if that was his real last name or just some kind of ironic nickname because he was a sort of loser. He'd really go on crying jags late at night. Anyway, one of Richard's bouncers, a man named Ken, apparently beat up Smiley pretty badly. Smiley was panhandling and he could get pretty terrifying, I have to admit. A couple of the other men from the shelter saw all this and told me about it. Apparently, Smiley went off on another bender because we haven't seen him since. Anyway, the night after the Smiley incident, I went over and confronted Richard. I did it three or four different nights, actually. Of course I knew that at least part of my anger was because he'd dumped me. By then I'd identified the species—the man who needs conquest. He'd really suckered me in and I'd thought he might truly be this lost little boy with the rough exterior. But I was just another conquest. He'd probably never seduced a Catholic social worker before."

"You didn't see him after that?"

"I probably entertained the foolish notion that he'd start missing me and would call but he never did. And I really was angry about the way his men had started pushing our people around."

"Do you remember where you were the night he was killed?"

"My God," she said.

"What's wrong?"

"You're asking me for an alibi."

"Not really. Just for a little information."

"I didn't kill him."

"That's probably the truth."

"'Probably.' Now that's reassuring." She shot me a cute frown. "I really want to like you, Jack. I really do."

"Couldn't you tell me where you were the other night and still like me?"

"I suppose."

"So?"

"So I was here."

"In your office?"

"In my office and working at the front door."

"What happens at the front door?"

"On very cold nights—and with the wind chill factor it was a hundred below the other night—they line up around the block. We have to do the worst thing of all—actually turn some people away. Anyway, we were so busy I had to come in and help."

"I see."

"So you're thinking that in all the chaos I could have easily slipped out and walked down the two alleys that lead to the Avanti's rear parking lot and killed him."

"I suppose it could have happened."

"It didn't. And I'm going to like you despite yourself."

"I appreciate that."

"In fact, in the nicest way you remind me of this man I've had two dates with over the past week."

"You seem to be on a roll."

"He's an Army Colonel. He wants me to think he's tough but he's actually very sensitive."

She fit the Avanti pattern—everybody there had too many lovers and too little peace. She was a woman of parts and as such scared me suddenly—I couldn't find the center that connected the Catholic social worker dumbstruck by the sight of a dead infant beneath a bed and a rather superficial young woman who'd pursue somebody as risky and dark as Richard Coburn.

I stood up and walked over to the door. "If I have any questions later, I'll call you."

"I wish you'd call me anyway. Or I guess I do. Don't you get confused sometimes like that?"

"What about the Colonel?"

"We're not engaged or anything, the Colonel and I."

I nodded. "Well, I've enjoyed talking with you."

"Me, too, Jack. Me, too." Then she glanced at her desk in such a way that I knew she wanted to get back to her work. "Well," she said, pushing me out the door, "see you."

"Right," I said. "See you."

I walked down to the end of the corridor, passing men in ragged but clean clothes smelling of soup and Aqua Velva. Somewhere in the building breakfast was being made. The air smelled of sausage and eggs.

About the time I reached the doors leading to the vestibule, I had the sense that somebody was watching me. I turned around. There were too many people in the corridor to find him at first. But finally his eyes burned through all else and I saw him, peeking around a corner, staring at me with unfathomable loathing—the "priest" I'd seen in the back of the Avanti the first morning I'd checked the security system over for Richard Coburn. This morning he was clean and shaved and wore a flannel shirt and wrinkled gray work trousers. He also wore his Roman collar. He looked no less insane than he had the other morning.

I pushed through the doors and went outside into sunny winter whiteness, the fumes of diesel fuel tart on the morning air.

For the next three hours I played boss at American Security. In high school, when I worked on loading docks and swept up grocery stores and detasseled corn on scorching summer farms, I always had the idea that it would be fun to be boss. You just sit back with your feet up on the desk and deal out fate like a poker dealer tossing out cards. Even when I was a cop, and should have known better, I thought that being a captain would be pretty cushy. No more freezing beats; no more heart-in-throat moments in dark alleys; no more emergency-room sorrows telling a sobbing woman that her drunken teenage son had died. Cushy job, being boss. But when I became the occasional substitute boss at American Security I learned the real facts. Being boss is no fun at all.

For the first hour that afternoon, I listened to three different fanciful stories about why three different workers couldn't make it in today—every excuse, it seemed, but being abducted by aliens. Then I took two calls from unhappy clients, the second one being especially acrimonious, a shopping mall manager who made up in ire what he lacked in literacy. Finally, and much as I didn't want to, I had Leonard Smythe come into my office, Leonard being the hapless security guard I was to fire if he was ever caught sleeping on the job again. Two employees reported finding Leonard asleep. My task was obvious.

He came in and said, "How they hangin', Mr. Dwyer?" which was his standard greeting, and then when he sat down he started picking his nose in a furtive annoying way and then sort of wiping it on the arm of the chair. He was apparently under the impression he was invisible. But just about the time I wanted to get up and go over and slap him around on general principles, I noticed for the first time the ketchup stain on his blue uniform shirt and I couldn't be mad at him anymore. Leonard was forty-three. He was thirty pounds overweight, bald, nearsighted, and he had breath that could peel paint. He was the big dumb clumsy kid who'd never grown up, much as he'd tried. These days the only assignments we could trust him with were patroling malls during business hours. We figured that all the traffic would keep him awake. But now he'd managed to screw up even that.

"God, Leonard," I said.

"You're pretty pissed, huh, Mr. Dwyer?"

"Yeah, Leonard, I guess I kind of am, you know?"

"That's what my wife said. That you were gunna really be pissed."

"I mean it's nothing personal, Leonard. You know that."

"I know, Mr. Dwyer. You've got your job to do and all that."

"Why did you go into the theater, Leonard? It wasn't on your beat."

"I just like Clint Eastwood, I guess. And the girl at the counter always lets me in free."

"You mean you've done this before?"

"Uh, yeah, Mr. Dwyer, I have. I mean, I don't usually sit down and fall asleep. Most of the time I just kind of pop my head in and see a few minutes of the movie and then go back to work. Kind of like a coffee break but I have Good and Plentys and a Coke instead, you know?"

"Right."

"Well, yesterday I was real tired on account of my wife's rash."

"Your wife's rash?"

"Yeah, she's had this rash on her back and she can't sleep. She's either trying to scratch it or she's asking me to scratch it. So neither one of us has been getting much sleep."

"Ah."

"So anyway yesterday I go in to see a few minutes of this Clint Eastwood movie and I sat down and bingo."

"Bingo?"

"Yeah, I fell asleep."

"Right."

"And when I woke up the movie was over."

"Didn't the girl try to wake you up?"

"She got off just about the time I went in. I guess the new girl just thought I was a regular customer."

I shook my head. "You know what the boss said the last time you fell asleep."

"Well."

"He said I'm supposed to fire you."

"I know, Mr. Dwyer."

I sighed. "Goddammit, Leonard."

"I know, Mr. Dwyer."

"Can't you drink a lot of coffee or something to stay awake?"

"Coffee always makes me pee like a racehorse."

"Well, how about caffeine pills or something?"

"They make me nauseous."

"Then maybe you should get some more sleep."

"Well—you know—the rash."

"Oh, right. I forgot. The rash."

"I don't blame you for being pissed, Mr. Dwyer. I don't blame you one bit."

"Has she gone to the doctor?"

"For her rash?"

"Right."

"Uh, no."

"Why not?"

"You know how much doctors charge for a visit these days? We just don't have that kind of money. Not unless we really get sick or something."

"Jesus Christ, Leonard."

"What is it, Mr. Dwyer?"

"This is making me fucking nuts. How much is a doctor visit?"

"Thirty-five dollars."

I took out my checkbook. I spelled his name right

and I made the amount thirty-five dollars.

"Aw, Mr. Dwyer. You shouldn't do this. It's your own money."

"It's a Christmas gift."

"God, Mr. Dwyer."

"Go call your wife and tell her you're going to pick her up and take her to the doctor's." I leaned forward. " Leonard, if I'd actually fired you, what the hell would you have done?"

"Moved in with my brother-in-law, I guess. He's got a good job on the line at Rockwell. But then my wife would really be in trouble."

"Why's that?"

"'Cause my brother-in-law's whole family has got this rash. That's where my wife picked it up from."

"I see."

"Jeez, they make me uncomfortable just bein' around them."

"Scratching, huh?"

"All the time."

"Go, Leonard. Call your wife. And stay awake, all right, Leonard?"

"You're one hell of a guy, Mr. Dwyer."

"Leonard, how many times have I asked you to call me Jack."

"Oh, yeah, right, Mr. Dwyer."

"Go, Leonard. Go."

He went.

The call came in an hour later. Male voice. Probably middle-aged. "Jack Dwyer, please."

"Speaking."

"You're the one who's been around the restaurant, right?"

"Around the Avanti?"

"Right."

"That's me."

"I wondered if we could talk."

"Would you give me your name, sir?"

"Sure. Harry Evans."

"And you work where, Mr. Evans?"

"At the restaurant."

"At the Avanti?"

"Yessir."

"I see."

"I've got a break in half an hour. I could meet you at the Hardees near Jackson Park."

"You don't want to talk on the phone?"

"I'd rather not."

"Any particular reason for that?"

"I worked in Intelligence when I was in the Army. I know how easy it is to tap a phone."

"You're calling from the Avanti?"

"Right."

"And you think it might be tapped?"

"Possibly."

What the hell was going on here?

"It will take me forty-five minutes to get to Jackson Park, Mr. Evans."

"That's all right. I'll go ahead and have some dinner."

"You work at a fancy place like the Avanti and

you eat at Hardees?"

He laughed. "It's like owning a candy store. Eventually, you get tired of chocolate."

"I guess that's a good point."

"Forty-five minutes, then."

12

On its roof, Hardees had a large revolving tree all green and red and blue and yellow in the darkness. From unseen speakers Elvis Presley sang "Blue Christmas." In the doorway a disheveled Santa was saying goodbye to the last of the day's tots, in this case a cute little blond girl clutching a doll big enough to be her twin. Up at the cash register, the Muzak Christmas music fought a radio that talked of bloody terrorist deaths in the Middle East and in New Jersey the gunning down of a young cop by a drug pusher. At the counter, middle-class people in parkas and topcoats and leather bombardier jackets bought chicken cutlet sandwiches and pork tenderloins and fries and some kind of synthetic milk shakes served by quick-stepping, clean-cut teenagers in brown polyester uniforms and matching caps. In the booths beyond, little kids were packed into one side while on the facing side sat their parents, exhausted from an afternoon of shopping, mother or father too tired to fix dinner, and consequently ending up here. From what I could see, all the little kids thought it was a swell idea.

Harry Evans turned out to be a chunky man in a brown suede car coat and a Notre Dame sweatshirt. He had a grip that would have made a bodybuilder proud and a beard that probably needed shaving twice a day—sort of like Richard Nixon's—and a certain lively contempt in his dark eyes. The world had let Harry down in some profound way and he was not about to forget it. He appeared to be in his mid-forties. He did not seem unduly impressed with me and of course, having taken Ph.D courses in low self-esteem, I immediately assumed the fault was mine and not his.

He sat at a booth near the rear door. He saw me looking around and waved me over. "You must be Dwyer."

I sat down.

"You're not eating?"

I shrugged. "Just coffee."

He said, "I want you to guarantee me I'm not going to get involved."

"First of all, Mr. Evans, if you knew much about me you'd know that there's nothing I can guarantee anybody about anything. I'm just a guy, all right? And secondly, if you don't want to get involved, why are you talking to me?"

"What I mean is, I don't want my name used. Is that possible?"

"With the police?"

"Right."

"Any special reason for that?"

"I did time."

"I see."

"B and E."

"Where?"

"Fort Madison." He shrugged. "That's behind me now. But you know how cops are."

"I used to be a cop."

"That's your problem."

I looked around. I wanted to be one of the little kids, stomach filled with cheeseburger and french fries and head filled with images of the real Santa coming down my chimney Christmas Eve.

"What I was trying to say," I said, "was that not all cops hate ex-cons."

"Most do."

I sighed. "Okay. Most do but not all. How's that?"

"Fine."

It was like debating in the goddamn United Nations.

"So you wanted to talk."

"Tomkins didn't kill Coburn."

"No?"

"No."

"You know that for sure?"

"For sure."

"How's that possible?"

"Because you know how Earle's supposed to have been seen out at Coburn's car?"

"Right."

"It wasn't Earle."

"Who was it?"

"Mrs. Coburn."

"How do you know that?"

"Because I saw her lift Earle's blast jacket and

hat. From a distance, the Coburn babe and Earle are about the same size and all."

"You have any special reason for telling me this?"

He smiled. "Yeah. Because I'm such a good citizen."

"I take it you don't like them."

"The people at the restaurant?"

"Right."

"I like the hired help fine. It's the owners and the customers I can't stand."

"So it's at least a possibility that you'd lie about them."

"It's a possibility, yeah. But I don't happen to be lying."

"You saw Coburn's wife, Deirdre."

"I saw Coburn's wife, Deirdre, take Earle's jacket and hat from a hook in one of the back hallways."

"And then what?"

"Huh?"

"Then what did she do with them?"

"Put them on and wore them out to her husband's car and killed him."

"You saw her do this?"

"No, but what the hell else do you think she did with them?"

"But you didn't see this?"

"You really are an asshole."

"I'm trying to help Earle."

"Yeah, it really sounds like it."

"You saw her take the jacket and hat but after that you don't know what happened."

"Well, not for sure but it's reasonable to assume—"

"We can't assume anything. The prosecuting attorney won't assume anything. He'll ask if you actually saw Deirdre Coburn wear the jacket and hat to the car and then kill her husband and we'd have to say no."

"He thought he was such hot stuff."

"Coburn?"

"Yeah. He always liked to play the big deal. You know, circulate among the customers and say hello. A lot of the women he was hitting on. One night he even managed to get one down in the basement. He was pretending to show her around the restaurant, you know? Anyway, he got her in the wine cellar and pumped her right on the spot. One of the busboys walked in on him and Coburn got so mad that later that night he slapped the busboy in front of everybody."

"This busboy didn't happen to be Earle Tomkins, did he?"

"Yeah."

"You're giving Earle a motive."

"I don't mean to."

"I know. But you are anyway," I said.

He shrugged.

"You don't like working for them?" I asked.

"Not especially."

"Then why you do it?"

"They pay me. I'm a working man. It's that simple."

"So who do you think killed him?" I said.

"Either she killed him or Tom Anton did. Him and Anton, they hated each other."

"If I need you to testify about the jacket and hat, you'll help me out?"

"You ever seen what a prosecutor does to an ex-con on the witness stand?" He sighed and looked down. "I'll consider it, I guess."

"You did a nice thing, calling me. Earle will appreciate it."

"He's a good kid."

I finished my coffee and stood up. "I guess I may as well go ask Deirdre Coburn about what you just told me."

"I'd love to be there and see that bitch squirm."

However justified his anger might be, it was repellent to see. Hatred is something none of us wears very well.

"Thanks again, Mr. Evans."

"I'm gonna get fired over this and you know what?"

"What?"

He flicked cigarette ashes into his empty coffee cup. "I don't give a shit. That's what."

When I reached my car in the parking lot, an apple-cheeked family was sliding on the ice and laughing. After Harry Evans's cold and lonely rage, the laughter was nice to hear.

13

From the backseat I took the phone book and looked up Richard Coburn's address. It was about where I'd expected him to live, on one of those private lanes newly cut from red rock and timber and what used to be open forest land before developers bought it up ten years earlier.

On the way out I saw several groups of carolers. They looked pretty in the darkness and the snow. A few times I even turned off the radio and rolled down the window so I could hear them.

I drove out past the old-money houses all alight with Christmas ornaments, up into the timbered hills where narrow blacktop roads wound in circles past white stables and brick mansions set far back from the road.

The Coburn house was in a deep, timber-rugged valley, and surrounded by an even more rugged stone wall. I parked on a hill above, a quarter mile away, killing my lights, letting my eyes adjust to the moonlight. The house was a sprawling Tudor of wood and the same quarry stone as the fence around it. The adjoining three-stall garage was closed up tight. Smoke came in thin gray twists from the chimney; no lights shone anywhere in the house. Against the full moon a silhouette hawk flew, opening its wings in an updraft, soaring past the golden circle then becoming invisible against the dark gray firmament.

From the glove compartment I took the Zeiss binoculars. I tugged on my gloves.

Seen close up, the house was just as dark. Once I thought I saw light behind the surface of glass on the westernmost window but it proved to be moonlight refracted through wind-tossed pines. Another time, checking out the screened-in porch behind the house, I thought I saw a dark shape moving against the screen but after long consideration through the binoculars, I decided I was looking at some kind of tall object covered in a tarpaulin. When the wind shook the screen, the object seemed to move.

I spent ten minutes scoping everything out. I had no idea what I was looking for—probably nothing. I took boyish pleasure in using the binoculars. I so seldom got a chance. The car was warm and pleasant and I was thinking of a Cary Grant–Irene Dunne movie I was planning to see on cable later and life at the moment did not seem so bad for a former altar boy who had lost his way for a time. Then I spotted the car.

Clever devil that he was, the driver had pulled the small dark Honda off the road to the east of the Coburns' entrance, behind a copse of pines. You had to look long and hard to see it. I had but barely. All I really got a glimpse of was the tail end and the rusted bumper and the license plates. I had no idea where the driver was or what he was doing here. I decided to go and find out. I slipped my .38 Smith and Wesson from the holster I kept under the seat, put the binoculars back in the glove compartment, got out, locked the car, and set off.

The night air was cold, already pinching my nostrils. Moonlight lay silver across the blue snow, covering everything. Downhill headlights wound around the curving road headed in the opposite direction. The car's engine sounded lonely laboring in the night.

When I got to the Honda, I hefted the .38 tighter and went along a windbreak of pines adjacent to the car. I came out ten yards ahead of the Honda so I could, approach from the front.

From the cover of some birch trees, I could see that the engine was shut off and the lights were off. For a time there was just the wind and the cold silty snow and the soft soughing of the pines in the moonlight. Nothing moved inside the car. I assumed that the driver had gone off somewhere and since the only house for at least a mile in any direction was Coburn's, it was logical to assume he'd gone to see Mrs. Coburn. But Mrs. Coburn didn't appear to be home.

I went back along the windbreak of pines. When I came even with the Honda, I stopped, pushed through the sweet-smelling pines, and then rushed the car, putting my .38 right against the windshield in case somebody popped up inside.

But as I could see immediately, he wasn't going to be popping up any time soon.

I got out my flashlight from my parka and shined it around inside.

He was probably mid-thirties, chunky, dressed in an inexpensive three-piece brown business suit. His yellow and brown patterned tie was a couple inches too wide to be fashionable any longer and the reddish hairpiece he wore looked as if it had been made from Astroturf. He had a pug nose and a wide solemn mouth and right now his eyes appeared to be brown though in daylight they could easily be green. He had a small birthmark on the jawline of his right cheek. He had been shot in the chest. Dark sticky blood covered him as if he'd spit it up in a messy accident.

The window on the passenger side of the small silver car was smashed and that made me curious. I walked around the Honda in deep snow and got my light on the silver spider-webbing of the smashed window. Blood was streaked down the door. I fixed the light on the rusted doorhandle. Blood was sticky there, too.

I put the light on the ground and followed the blood along the snow, trying to find where he'd first been shot. I followed the blood out to the road and down to the entrance of the Coburn estate. The blood ended in dirty snow there. Apparently, he had been standing by the mailbox when he was shot and had turned to run back to his car. At several points you could see where he'd fallen and then gotten up to keep running back to his car. Since there were no other footprints, I assumed the killer had not followed him. There was a good chance that the killer had believed the man was dead right there at the mailbox and had therefore fled.

Back at the Honda, I set the light to working inside the car. There wasn't much to see. On the backseat was a small stack of four-color brochures and next to that stack another one of larger versions of the same brochure. A brown double-knit sportcoat inside its clear plastic laundry bag hung from a knob on the back window. From the rearview mirror dangled a St. Christopher's medal, which would make sense given the ruby Knights of Columbus ring he wore on his right hand. Nothing very helpful.

I took a break and went over and peed in the snow by the pines. Death, whether I admit it to myself or not, always scares me, and for a simple enough reason. Someday that will be me in the front seat of the Honda or slumped there in the armchair or drawing my last in the snug white hospital bed. As I peed, I listened to the wind in the pines, and smelled the tangy cones, and looked at the snow made blue by the night sky, and saw the brilliant stars. He was beyond all these pleasures now, the man in the car.

I decided to hell with it and opened the door from the driver's side.

He kept his car registration in a neat little deal on the other side of his visor. His name was Brian Ingram. I wrote down all the particulars and then reached into the backseat and grabbed a couple of the brochures which belonged to the Ardmore Chemical Company. With so many of them— maybe as many as fifty apiece—the brochures must belong to the company he worked for.

He stank pretty bad by now, so I was happy to close the door and stand in the clean cold air and look at the stars and wonder as always what the hell they meant and who put them there and why exactly. By the time I got done wondering I had to pee again, so I went back to the pines and did my dirty deed, and then I set off up the road, my work shoes loud against the gravel in the quiet night, and a dog somewhere complaining that I was disturbing his peace.

I got in my car and fired her up and got a good loud party station on the radio and then I drove at reasonable speed back to the city and found a phone booth and put in a call to 911 about where a body could be found in a certain Honda and hung up and went home.

14

I spent twenty minutes in the shower. First I shaved and then I got lathered up and then I turned the water so hot it nearly hurt.

In the bedroom I took a laundry-starched white shirt from its package and added a blue regimental-striped tie to it. I took a blue blazer and gray slacks from the closet and added black socks and black loafers to those and then I was ready to go. It was not a night to be sitting home alone.

I was reaching for my topcoat when the phone rang.

"Well, Dwyer, I'm being faithful. How about you?"

I laughed. Neither of us are exactly trusting people. While such suspicion embarrassed me, Donna never had any trouble expressing it.

"Just sitting here with two blondes," I said.

"Actually, that's just how I picture you. I suppose one is a stewardess and the other is a brain surgeon. For balance."

"Yes, and one thinks I'm very cute and the other thinks I'm very handsome."

"So have you been thinking about me?"

"About forty percent of the time. Have you been thinking about me?"

"About forty-two percent of the time."

"I guess you win."

"That's because I have a pure heart." Beat. "So have you really been faithful, Dwyer?"

"Uh-huh."

"Boy, that sounds definitive."

"I have been faithful. How's that?"

"Better."

"Are you enjoying the convention?"

"Parts of it are all right. But the kids kind of scare me."

"The kids?"

"The young ambitious ones. They have dead eyes. Like cokeheads. You know?"

"I know."

"At lunch the other day two of them pulled out this huge BMW brochure and started passing it around the table. It was disgusting."

"What did you do?"

"Went back to my room and read Graham Greene. He's so good."

"Yes, he is."

Beat. "I'll bet I miss you more than you miss me."

"Bet you don't."

Sigh. "I wish we were in my apartment and I was making dinner for us."

"Me, too."

"You think we'll ever get married?"

"I don't know. What do you think?"

"I thought we agreed to never answer a question with another question."

"Ah. I forgot about that particular pact."

"You could always get on a plane and come out here."

I told her about the Avanti and Coburn's murder. Instead of inquiring about the case, she said, "I suppose there are a lot of women at the Avanti."

"A few."

"And probably attractive ones, too."

"If you like them burly with three eyes."

Laughter. "Uh-huh."

"And speaking of the Avanti, that's just where I was going."

"Gee, what a subtle hint."

"So I'll pick you up at the airport three days from now at four-fifteen. "

"Right." Pause. "I'm sorry I'm not more trusting."

"Your ex-husband didn't give you much reason to be trusting."

"Thanks for saying that. I love you, Dwyer."

"And I love you." Pause. "I miss you, Donna. I heard carolers tonight and I thought of you. How much you'd have liked them."

"Boy, that was the perfect thing to say."

"Then I'd better hang up before I blow it by saying the wrong thing. Good night."

"Good night, Dwyer. Be good."

I didn't have to ask what she meant by that.

15

A huge Christmas tree had been set up to the right of the band. Multicolored holiday lights splashed over the dancers in the darkness as the band played "My Funny Valentine" and "Stairway to the Stars." It was not unlike a prom, and there was a real melancholy to it, as if everyone shared the secret knowledge that tomorrow morning the world would end.

Even more than usual, the Avanti looked like the set from a gangster picture made in the Forties. The platoon of waiters and captains, the photographer passing among the tables, and the tuxedoed men with sleek hair did not exactly discourage this impression.

I sat at the bar, three quick scotches warm in my stomach, and a plastic-tipped cigarillo wafting blue smoke between my fingers. I've managed to convince myself that smoking cigarillos—I try not to inhale them—is not smoking. Not exactly.

Thus far tonight I had seen no one I'd come to see—neither Mrs. Richard Coburn nor Mr. Richard Coburn's mistress, Jackie, nor the sleek Tom Anton nor his gorgeous daughter, Mignon.

"Another, sir?"

"Please."

The bartender, male, balding, neuter in some inoffensive way, nodded and vanished and reappeared and slid me my drink and took his money from the twenty and some change I'd left on the bar from the first drinks.

She said, "You look so handsome I hate to see you ruin it."

Jackie. She wore a dark green dress with a dramatic V-neck and her hair swept back so artfully that Scarlett O'Hara would probably be envious.

She guided my hand to the ashtray and smashed out the cigarillo. It was as if I were five years old and doing something naughty. I didn't mind at all.

"Alone?" she said.

"Always."

"Good."

I stood up so she could sit down. She nodded to the bartender. He knew exactly what she wanted. She said, "Maybe we were wrong the other night."

"About not going to your place?"

She nodded.

"No," I said, "we weren't wrong. I'm in love with somebody else."

"True-blue Dwyer."

"I try."

She sighed and smiled at the bartender as he set her drink down. "So do I. I was always faithful to Richard. I just wish he'd been to me."

I sipped my drink.

She said, "It was approval. That's what he wanted. I mean, I don't think he suffered from satyriasis or anything. But he did need approval. From men he got envy. He took pleasure in taking things away from them—their money or their businesses or their women."

"Nice guy."

"As I said the other night, Richard was a surprisingly nice guy. When he wasn't playing his 'war games' as he always called them. Taking things from people."

"What did he take from you?"

She laughed. "My good sense. I'm a very sensible girl, really. But for some reason around Richard—I mean, I should have said goodbye to him a long time ago. What did I get from it? At first, he couldn't even make love. But I stuck with him. And of course as soon as his sexual powers came back to him, he started cheating on me."

"Why did you stay with him?"

"He was the big violent boy I've always wanted."

"Really?"

"Really. He brought out something in me that was terrible and maternal at the same time. And then there were those moments when he was the sweetest man I've ever known. Sometimes when we'd lie in the dark, even his voice would change and I'd think that he was somebody else."

"His other women didn't bother you?"

I watched her reaction carefully.

"Still looking for a motive, aren't you? For why I may have killed him."

"I suppose."

"Don't you ever get tired of being a detective?"

"All the time."

"Why don't you quit, then?"

"Why didn't you dump Richard?"

Rather than answer me, she slid down from the stool and held out her arms.

"My God," I said, "you really are a masochist."

"Maybe you've taken dancing lessons since the last time I saw you."

"Dreamer."

On the floor her dress rustled as we moved through the steps of the fox trot. Her perfume was overmuch in a satisfying way and her breasts against me felt much better than I wanted them to. "I wish they'd play Christmas songs," she said. "I love it when the tree lights flash on and off and they play 'White Christmas' or 'I'll Be Home for Christmas.' Do you have a favorite Christmas song?"

" 'Blue Christmas.' "

"I like that, too."

"By Elvis."

She laughed. "Sure."

"I'm serious."

"You really like his version?"

"It's great."

"My, my," she said. "You are full of surprises, aren't you?" Then she held me tighter and we sort of swung around the floor, almost daring in our clumsiness. As we got closer to the trees, the lights played against her dark hair. She was from another era, the time when women didn't always count calories or worry about job promotions or consider a man too demanding because he wanted to spend

all his time with her, at least during that heady period of sexual and emotional excess that marks the
start of most affairs. I didn't know if I even liked
women like that anymore but somehow with the
snow failing again and the night bitter cold and
Donna gone, it was comfortable in her arms, middle-aged comfortable even though she wasn't yet
thirty, and so I watched the lights play off her hair
and loved it.

"Oh, God," she said.

"What?"

"Look who's here."

I followed her gaze to the bar. Deirdre Coburn,
in a black dress and a great deal of jewelry, sat at
the bar watching us dance.

"She killed him," Jackie said.

"Is that just a guess or do you have some facts?"

"He spent all her money."

"How?"

"Here. The Avanti. She always pretends to have
so much. Her father was a very successful lawyer.
He had a great deal of money—a lot of which he
cheated his clients out of, I'm told—but he had a very
bad drinking problem and squandered most of it."

"What about Earle Tomkins?"

"Earle didn't kill him."

"Nobody seems to think so but the police." I
didn't want to tell her what I'd learned about
Deirdre Coburn stealing Tomkins's clothes.

She held me tight again. Deirdre glowered at us
then turned back to the bar, jamming her cigarette

out and swallowing her drink quickly. With a long arm, she pointed languidly to the bartender. Apparently this was some kind of sign language for another drink.

Jackie said, "And now the night's complete. Tom Anton and his strange little daughter."

"You don't like Mignon?"

"Something's wrong with her. I'm probably being unfair."

"Wrong with her?"

"Problems of some kind. She used to come in here during the day sometimes and she'd hardly speak to me. But the longer I watched her, the more I sensed that she must have some kind of head problems."

"But no idea what?"

She nuzzled into me. "Don't you ever get tired of talking?"

"I'm interested in your theories. What kind of problems could Mignon have?"

She nuzzled me again and sighed. "I'm afraid I can't help you. It's just the way she acts—she's just strange. Now come on. Dance with me."

So we danced. Only once—well, maybe twice—did she make one of those involuntary little squeals that meant I'd tromped on her foot again. I would probably be opening up a studio soon and giving lessons.

When the orchestra quit, the lights coming up for a break, we turned and went back to our table. Deirdre and Tom and Mignon stood along the bar, watching us.

"They really like me." Jackie laughed as I held her seat for her. "They just hide it well."

For the next forty minutes there was a floor show, a smutty comic who had stolen the mannerisms of five famous comedians and didn't know what to do with any of them. We drank and I ordered a steak sandwich and it came and I asked if I would be permanently barred from the place if I put ketchup on the meat and she said to be her guest and so I did and not more than ten people sitting around us sent over imperious disapproving glances. Maybe it was the way I pounded on the upside-down ketchup bottle with the heel of my hand. All this time, Jackie ate delicately from her salmon steak. She even gave me a couple of bites. The stuff was good, no doubt about it.

Just after the comic left and the lights went down again and the glow of the Christmas tree came up, Jackie excused herself and went to the ladies' room and Deirdre Coburn came over and stood by her chair.

"I hope you're not charging me for tonight," she said. "Because I won't pay for it."

"Calm down, Mrs. Coburn."

"You bastard, who do you think you're kidding, anyway? You're supposed to be proving that she killed him and here you are dancing with her."

"Why don't we try that?"

"Try what?"

But by then I was up and escorting her to the dance floor. She resisted at first but I kept moving. On the floor she relented and put her slender arm on my shoulder and we started in.

"Jesus," she said almost immediately.

"What's wrong?"

"You stepped on my foot."

"Ah."

So we danced some more and I tried very hard not to step on her foot. It was not the same with her in the Christmasy darkness as it had been with Jackie.

"It's my understanding that you took Earle Tomkins's jacket and hat the night of the murder."

"What are you talking about?"

There was just enough light to see her face and in her face I could see she was lying.

She said, "God."

"You admit it then?"

"I thought you were working *for* me." She sighed. "Could we go to Richard's office?"

She served brandy in snifters. I sat in a deep leather chair and stared at a fireplace that looked cold and dark as death. She sat dramatically on the edge of his mahogany desk and stared for a long moment at the floor-to-ceiling bookcases. I'd checked them out—just the sort of stuff the real Jay Gatsby probably read, all about how to be number one and then a lot more books on how to remain number one.

She said, "Who told you?"

"It isn't important."

"Of course it's important."

"I'm not going to tell you so we may as well drop it." I hesitated. "Why did you take his jacket and hat?"

She sighed. "So if anybody saw me, they'd think I was Earle. We're about the same size and all bundled up that way, nobody could tell it was me. Especially Richard."

"So you went out to his car bundled up and pretending to be Earle and you killed him?"

"Killed him? Don't be ridiculous. I went out to his car to see if I could find something. I didn't want Richard to know that I knew he had it."

"Had what?"

"Some kind of report."

"What kind of report?"

"That's what I was trying to figure out." She took a long drag from her cigarette and blew blue smoke to the tiled ceiling. "Two days before he died, a tacky little man dropped something off here at the restaurant. He said it was a report Richard was waiting for. I happened to be at the bar. The man gave it to Earle and Earle took it and put it in Richard's office. Richard was at one of the country clubs, impressing everybody with his importance. Anyway, I didn't think anything of it, but when Richard got back and saw it, he got very sullen and angry."

"But you don't know what was in the report?"

"No. Just that it changed his mood abruptly. He'd been very happy the two days previous because he was lining up investors for another restaurant he'd own entirely on his own. He wanted to be away from all of us—me, Tom, even Jackie, though I'm not sure she knew that."

"Did you ever see the envelope close up?"

"No. I just remember that it had the name of some chemical company on it."

"I'd like you to tell me what happened the night you put on Earle's clothes and went out to Richard's car."

"Nothing happened."

"Nothing?"

"The car was locked. I couldn't get in."

"Why did you think that the envelope was in the car anyway?"

"Because I'd seen him carry it out there along with other things. Richard often did that. Carried things out and set them in the car. Then he'd come back in for a last drink or something."

"So Richard wasn't there when you got there?"

"No."

"And the car was locked?"

"Yes."

"When the police found Richard's body, the door on the driver's side was open and some of Richard's blood was on the seat."

"Yes. Proving that I didn't kill him."

"Jesus," I said.

"What?"

"You're some prize, you know that?"

"Meaning what exactly, Mr. Dwyer?"

"Meaning that you're letting Earle Tomkins take the blame for your husband's death."

"I knew the police would eventually find out who really killed him."

"Your faith in our justice system is touching, Mrs. Coburn."

"You're sounding as if you don't like me anymore, Mr. Dwyer."

"Tonight I want you to call a detective named Cummings at the third precinct and tell him what you did the night of Richard's murder."

"I really wouldn't have let Earle stay in there long."

"The detective's name is Cummings. C-u-m-m-i-n-g-s."

For the next few minutes we sat there glaring at each other. I thought of Earle and his poor mother.

"Why did you want the envelope anyway?"

"I wanted to see what was in it."

"Why?"

"Because I thought I could get some of my power back. Don't you know, dear, that's what bitches like me spend their time doing. Getting power. I used to run Richard's life. But then he got so embarrassed about his poor sexual performance that he had to turn elsewhere—and then I didn't have any power over him whatsoever."

"And he'd already spent all your money."

She smirked. "You've been talking to Jackie again. Did you know her mother was a maid at a Holiday Inn?"

"Richard got some letters over the past few months. Do you know anything about them?"

"Would you like some more brandy?"

"No. Tell me about the letters."

"He burned them one night. Very dramatically. I came into the den and there he was weaving around in front of the fireplace. He could barely stand up. Then he took three or four white envelopes and tossed them into the fire."

"You don't know who sent them or what they were about?"

"No."

"I want you to tell me about the man who gave Earle the report."

"You're getting very good at giving orders. Particularly in light of the fact you're my employee."

"The man."

She went over and got more brandy from a cut glass decanter. "He was just a man."

"Height."

"Oh, I don't know."

"Tall, short, medium?"

"Medium."

"Color of hair?"

She laughed. "I suppose that depended on which toupee he wore on a given day. He wore a very cheap rug. I was almost embarrassed for him."

"Did you get a look at his face?"

"His face?"

"Yes, Mrs. Coburn, his face."

"Oh. Yes. He had a—birthmark or something on his right cheek."

Now there could be no doubting who we were talking about. By now the police would have packed Brian Ingram in an ambulance and shipped him out for an autopsy.

I stood up. "Remember to call Cummings."

"I believe you mentioned that."

"If he's not at work ask for his home number. Tell them it's an emergency and they'll give it to you."

"I really wasn't going to let Earle sit in jail, Mr. Dwyer."

"Right," I said. "Right." I left.

The commotion came from someplace in the kitchen. Pans and pots clanged as they bounced off tiled flooring. Shouts and curses erupted like gunfire. All I could do was run forward, pulled by the noise.

Pushing through the kitchen doors, I saw a short man with a corny little mustache putting his hands to his mouth in shock. He wore the big white hat of the head chef.

"What's going on?" I said. But before he could answer I saw, down a long corridor and in spill light from the back door, a man in a dinner jacket laying punches into a scrawny, scarecrow form that looked familiar to me.

"There ain't no reason to kill him," the chef said. "Ain't" sounded very wrong coming from a man in a big chef's hat.

Other kitchen help had gathered around, staring down the corridor. At another time the kitchen with its multiple stoves and ovens and endless overhead jungle of hanging utensils would have been impressive. Now all I noticed, in a quick glimpse, was how dirty and wet the floors were and how sour some of the food smelled cooking.

I ran down the small corridor. By the time I reached the man doing the punching I saw that it was my old friend Ken from the other night. He glanced my way and frowned.

"Let him go," I said, nodding to the freaky man who'd been wearing the Roman collar in the alley the other day.

The back door was open and probably had been most of the night. The kitchen heat was numbing. So you open a door and a derelict wanders in and—

But you don't beat him this way.

I hit Ken as hard as I could just above the ear. I had the pleasure of hearing his skull crack against the wall on the other side of the door.

The freaky man got up from his crouch. He wore just a white T-shirt, stained now with his own blood, gray wrinkled work pants, and green high-top tennis shoes. I wondered how badly he'd been hurt. Blood flowed from the side of his mouth. He managed to look both terrified and indifferent. I pointed to the screen door behind him. "Get the hell out of here. Now."

I caught the flick of his eyes in the shadows— just soon enough to duck the roundhouse Ken aimed at me.

Ken's fist landed squarely against the wall. I could hear the knuckles pop and shatter. He looked almost silly, a bulky guy in an expensive black dinner jacket, with baby fine blond hair combed neatly like a 1959 fraternity boy and this big gorilla torso, waggling a big painful hand.

But you should not underestimate 1959 fraternity boys.

I was moving in for one last punch—we definitely did not like each other—when I saw and heard, more or less simultaneously, a switchblade appear in his left hand. The blade flashed out.

I was scared. I shouted, "Call the police!"

But he wasn't going to give me time. He forced me back against the door frame and started moving the knife in ever closer swipes past my windpipe.

I considered talking to him, saying Hey, pal, the most either of us are going to get out of this is a fine for assault. But a knife, my friend—

But he wasn't my friend, of course, and as he lunged for me, I rolled away, scrambling back up the short corridor to the kitchen proper.

The people in white jackets moved out of my way, all the time, yelling "Watch it!"

I wasn't sure what they were talking about until I felt his foot crash against my ankle and knock my own feet out from under me, sending me into a kind of swan dive for the red tiled floor that was all dirty from winter footprints.

Before I could find my feet again, he kicked me

twice in the ribs and once in the stomach. He must have been a fullback at one time or the other.

When the help started yelling, "Watch it!" again I started yelling back. "Hit him with something for Christ's sake!" A single glance had told me that he'd gone crazy in some irredeemable way. Thorazine was about the only thing that was going to bring this guy back.

The knife blade got the shoulder of my blazer and tore it halfway down my sleeve. Fortunately, he'd managed to tear jacket and shirt without getting my flesh.

I dove for his knees, startling him enough to back him up against a stainless steel refrigerator. I brought a punch straight up to his groin. While he was dealing with the pain of that, I got to my feet.

Feeling I was in the clear, I started to move away from him but the onlookers started yelling again. This time I wasn't so lucky. His knife blade caught me right across the back of the neck. The pain was overwhelming, dizzying. I staggered against the stainless steel refrigerator door, trying to make sure that I stayed on my feet.

The yelling got intense again.

I turned back to him and saw him lunging at me. At that moment he looked bigger than he ever had. His madness was palpable now, a madness particular to the male of the species, the sort that leads men to open fire on twenty SWAT-team members, knowing that they have no more than ten seconds to live and not giving one damn at all.

This time he brought the knife up in an arc and then back down. He was aiming for the area of my heart. He meant to do fatal damage.

Moving away from the refrigerator, I trailed a hand behind me. I felt the edge of something very hot. When I glanced backward with one eye, I saw two bays in a wide deep-fat fryer. The foot-deep grease was boiling.

He didn't see it in time.

I let him come in waving the blade, holding still as long as my nerve would last, and then at the final moment I stepped aside and grabbed his knife hand and pushed it deep into the fryer.

I'd thought I might take some pleasure in the noise of his scream. But there was just fear and useless rage and pain in his voice and I knew these things too well to take any genuine pleasure in inflicting them on anyone else.

I shouted in his ear, "I'll pull your hand out if you leave the knife down there. If you don't, I'll put your face in the grease next time. Do you understand?"

But he was in too much pain to say anything coherent. For good measure I slapped him once very hard across the mouth with my free hand, just the way he'd been slapping the homeless man around.

"You hear what I said about the knife?"

"Please," he said, "Please." He could barely talk. His eyes ran with tears. His plump pink mouth trembled.

I took his hand out.

To the chef I said, "Tell the cops I'll file a complaint against this jerk sometime tonight. Right now I'm going to try and find somebody."

I grabbed a clean towel from the chef's hand, sopped it against my neck, fixing it like a collar, and took off running.

16

Moonlight threw the tops of the alley buildings into black relief against the dark blue sky. Somewhere ahead of me I heard a human mewling, and ice crunched under the weight of stumbling feet.

I pushed on into the gloom, still hearing him perhaps a hundred yards ahead but unable to make out even his silhouette. Only when he reached the mouth of the alley and turned right was I able to glimpse him at all.

I ran, sliding on the ice, keeping my arms out straight for balance. On either side of me the aged backsides of the buildings brought back other eras, recalling those days when I'd pedaled my Schwinn down just such fascinating alleys as these where contraband Lucky Strikes could be smoked without your parents knowing, and nude women could be glimpsed in the photography magazine stolen from somebody's older brother, and you could sit smelling the sweet scents of the bakery a couple hundred feet away and pore leisurely through the newest issue of *Amazing Stories* or *Manhunt*.

When I reached the head of the alley, I, too, turned right, only I didn't see him. Ahead of me stretched a deserted back street, the nearest part dimly lighted from a streetlight but the rest of it lost in darkness. I stopped, panting, listening. At first I heard the expected city sounds—cars, a distant ambulance, chatter. But then I heard the odd mewling sound he'd been making. The sound was close by.

Ahead of me, on my right, was a vast four-story warehouse. Vandals had smashed all the windows and graffiti artists had covered it with their ironies and rage. It sat sprawling and dead, a testament to the days when Rust Belt buildings such as these had pounded with the energy and purpose of American industry. This was long before the Germans and the Japanese decided to take over America by stealth rather than violence, and we decided to let them.

I walked toward him carefully. I wanted to talk to him. I was afraid he'd bolt like a terrified animal. It didn't help that I couldn't see him. He was somewhere on the side of the building in the shadows. I gave him plenty of warning, my breath still pitching ragged, my feet snapping ice underfoot.

I saw his eyes first. Even in the shadows they retained their mad clarity. He was huddled next to a door holding his stomach from the beating Ken had given him. Every few seconds, seeming timed to every other exhalation or so, he made the mewling sound.

"You should go back to St. Mark's," I said. "Have them check you."

He drew up tighter to the doorway.

"I'm not going to hurt you, all right?"

He said nothing. Just watched me.

"A few weeks ago the restaurant had trouble with somebody coming in the back door. I need to know if that was you." My voice had a loud, ridiculous ring to it. Neither of us were dressed for winter, yet here we were, conversing. Or rather, here I was trying to converse.

"You can hear me all right, can't you?"

The eyes widened. A little whiter. After a moment, he nodded. "Why have you been sneaking into the restaurant?"

He said, "Smiley was my friend. They beat him up." He spoke slowly haltingly, as if with great pain. "Smiley" was the derelict Gwen Daily had mentioned as disappearing. I wondered why he'd mentioned Smiley. He said nothing else.

"I'm not going to tell the police anything. I just want to know. A man was murdered the other night and I have the feeling that you can help me find out who killed him."

I started blowing on my hands and rubbing my arms to stay warm. "I'm sorry Ken beat you. You didn't deserve that, even if you did sneak in."

He continued to stare. His eyes gave the impression that he was listening, evaluating.

"I want to ask you a question and I'd appreciate an answer, all right?"

He said nothing, of course.

"The man who was killed the other night—did you kill him?"

He said nothing, of course.

"Why have you been sneaking into the restaurant?"

He said, "Behold, the Lord God helps me; who will declare me guilty?"

I sighed. We were back to Bible quotations.

Abruptly, his head jerked. He heard them before I did. In the frozen night their pounding feet had the sound of terrible authority.

"They're looking for both of us," I said.

He scrambled to his feet but almost immediately doubled over and began mewling again. I went over to him and touched his shoulder. Even in the senses-numbing cold, he smelled sour.

Back at the restaurant he'd taken several hard shots to the belly. There could have been serious damage. "You'd better have somebody check you over soon," I said, when he straightened up again. "Do you understand?"

He nodded.

"Do you know a back way out of here?"

He nodded again.

"Then you'd better take it because they're going to be here in a minute or so."

He stared at me. "Happy is he who is kind to the poor."

I smiled. "I sure hope that's true, my friend. I sure hope that's true."

By now their shouts, close up, were loud and coarse. "Hurry up, now," I said.

Then he was gone, one with the shadows and the night, vanished. I suppose that's one of the many tricks street people learn to survive.

And then they were there. Two of them, beefy

and shiny with sweat, wore dinner jackets with cute
little bow ties. These, of course, were Ken's fellow
bouncers. The third man surprised me—it was
Tom Anton. He was so languidly handsome you
wouldn't have thought running was in him.

While Ken's friends glowered at me, Anton said,
"Did you get him?"

"Get who?"

"The bastard who's been sneaking into the restaurant." He was out of breath and sounded
vaguely as if he were going to be sick.

"No."

"No? What do you mean, no?" He'd started
mistaking me for an employee again.

The four of us stood near the curb in the dirty
street light. A Lincoln Continental went by on its
quick crushing way out of the ghetto and the passengers, obviously recognizing Anton, gawked.

I said, "Anton, I don't have to put up with any
more of your bullshit."

"I wasn't giving you any bullshit."

"I know. I guess you probably talk to everybody
that way."

"I want you to find that man."

"Why?"

"Why? Why do you think why? Because he's been
sneaking into the restaurant."

I studied his glistening face. "A man wanders in
a few times from the street, probably to get food,
and everybody at the restaurant gets violently upset. That seems pretty strange to me."

"It does? Then you wouldn't mind if somebody wandered around inside your business?"

I nodded to the tuxedo twins. "I wouldn't hire goons to beat him up."

He shrugged. "Apparently you don't know much about cocaine. Enough of our clientele use it that we have problems from time to time—psychotic episodes." He indicated the two men with his noble chin. "These men do a very good job of keeping things peaceful."

"Yeah, like beating up some poor bastard who can barely walk anyway."

"Ken gets carried away sometimes. And anyway, who're you to talk, Dwyer? You pushed his arm into the deep-fat fryer."

"Be sure to mention that in his hand he had a knife."

He shook his head. "Dwyer, this is a very confused time for me. Whether you believe it or not, Richie and I were good friends at one time. His death has upset me. I want to find out who killed him—if it wasn't Earle Tomkins." He shrugged. "Deirdre told me what she did—taking Earle's jacket and cap and pretending to be him—and I know that sounds suspicious but you didn't know Richie very well. He would have killed her if he'd caught her snooping around his car. He had a violent temper." He shuddered. The sweat was drying. He was getting cold.

"Ducky," I said. "Deirdre hires me to prove that Jackie did it. Jackie hints that Deirdre did it. Now who are you going to blame?"

The tuxedo twins looked angry that I'd talk to their boss in such a way.

Anton shook his head and said, "You're hopeless."

I half-expected him to say ciao.

They left, the three of them, the two in tuxedos glaring at me over their shoulders. Then I was alone in the ragged, rusted-out neighborhood, and another fancy car, this time a long gray Audi, passed by, the dowager in the driver's seat shaking her head at the sight of me. I probably looked disheveled and crazed but I still resented her glance.

In the alley again, the cost of my twenty-minute exposure to the cold beginning to take its toll, I heard a faint squeaking, almost the peeping you associate with little yellow chicks on Easter Sunday.

But somehow I knew who and what it was.

"Well, I'll be damned," I said, leaning down and finding her scrawny little body in the darkness. "It's you again, isn't it, sweetie?"

It was the little tabby kitty I'd picked up my first day on the job at the restaurant. Then I'd put her trembling into the pocket of my topcoat. Now, I held her up in the moonlight and got a good look at her tiny sweet face, the huge grave eyes, the birdy little mouth that peeped every once in a while. I thought of what horrors she must go through minute by minute, hour by hour, day by day, struggling against the elements and predators in an indifferent world. She'd never last the night. Not this subzero night.

"I'll bet you're as cold as I am, aren't you, hon?" She peeped. I had to interpret that as an affirmative.

So I decided to do it. I eased her down in the pocket of my blazer and kept my hand in there to keep her as warm as possible.

When I got back inside the restaurant to pick up my topcoat, Jackie said, "The last time I saw you, I was headed for the ladies' room for a quick pit stop. I just assumed you'd wait for me. But Deirdre told me you've been busy."

"You're friends with Deirdre now?"

She frowned. "Death makes strange bedfellows. Deirdre and Tom and I have something in common now, I guess. We had a talk last night. Somebody we cared about very much has died."

My little friend made her peeping sound.

We were in the lobby of the restaurant. The maitre d's head snapped to attention when he heard the faint kitty noise.

"What've you got in there?" Jackie asked.

I let the kitty stick her head up. She looked around, marveling.

"A cat," Jackie said.

"Right."

"I hate cats."

"Ah."

"The whole idea of litter boxes disgusts me."

"I'm sorry."

The maitre d' was on his way over. He was probably going to report me to some senate committee on bad taste or something.

"See you," I said to Jackie.

I left.

At my apartment I put a towel inside a cardboard box and I heated a bowl of skim milk and set it inside the box and then I put the tabby inside on the towel. She lapped at the milk so heartily that she got tired every thousand slurps or so and would take a brief rest break. Then, sighing, she'd go back at it again.

I got in bed and lay in darkness. I couldn't sleep. For a time I stared at the way the streetlight made the frosted window golden. Wind rattled the window and snowlike grains of sand blew against the glass. I thought of Donna mostly and then I was thinking of my kids when I felt a tiny warm paw touch my cheek.

I picked her up and put her under the covers and she lay with her head on the edge of the pillow and went promptly to sleep.

Soon after, I joined her.

17

In the morning I went to the 7-Eleven and got kitty litter and a kitty box and came back and fixed up my new friend. She spent the first five minutes timidly walking around inside the box, pawing at the litter but leaving it fresh. Finally, I gave her a kiss on top of the head and left.

The motel I wanted, the one where Richard Coburn supposedly spent so much time, was located on the northeast edge of the city, where planners expect the building boom to last well into the next century. Even in the overcast light of day, the place looked impressive, all natural woods and stone and glass. It looked like anything but a motel, the rooms hidden behind the set-like front of the place.

Inside, I had to pass by a wide blue pool that smelled of chlorine. In the lapping water a woman with a pretty face and wonderful middle-aged breasts played with two young kids while her husband sat in a lounge chair smoking a cigar and reading the *Wall Street Journal*.

At the desk a young man who appeared to have graduated from training school about twenty minutes ago made his voice deep as possible and said, "Good morning, sir. May I help you?" He sounded like a Marine recruit facing a psychotic drill instructor.

"The manager, please."

"Mr. Farnsworth?"

"If he's the manager."

"May I tell him who's calling?" All this time he kept a grin on his face. I wanted to give him a tranquilizer. I supposed my own son would be going through all this soon enough, the rough passage into the world of real jobs.

I handed over a card.

"You're a detective?" His voice cracked on the last word.

Two or three people who'd been standing around watching the woman with the nice face and the wonderful breasts now shifted their attention to me. The kid sure knew how to keep things quiet.

I leaned in so I could whisper. "Why don't you just go tell Mr. Farnsworth I'd like to see him?"

Understanding that he was being chastised, he flushed. "Yessir."

And went away to return about two minutes later, during which time I traded smiles with the two salesmen-types who kept looking me over. So this is what a real detective looks like, huh? Gee, what a disappointment. He didn't even shoot anybody.

"Mr. Farnsworth said all right."

I turned back to the kid, my eyes having become almost permanently fixed on the woman in the water, and said, "Down that hallway?"

"Yessir."

"Thank you."

"Yessir." He was very tight now and he didn't

like me worth a damn. He had too much pride for a kid his age.

The hall smelled of chlorine right up to where I reached a heavy, carved wooden door. I knocked with a single knuckle and a rumbling bass voice told me to come in.

The office was wide and done in leather and mahogany and big framed photographs of various state university football players. On his desk was a stand-up plaque in the shape of a football with the state colors saying I'M A BOOSTER AND PROUD OF IT. Much as I like state football, all this stuff embarrasses me. The owners of this paraphernalia always manage to come on like the worst kind of teenagers; it seems to freeze them in gawky adolescence. And maybe that's exactly why they do it. Beer parties forever.

"Mr. Dwyer?"

I stuck my hand across the desk. Farnsworth was a beefy, bald man with mean blue eyes. He had a grip that meant to impress and did. As he sat down, he tucked his red power tie inside his blue power suit. He sat back and brought thick hands into a prayerful position. He wore two big diamond rings and a sneer. I doubted that Mr. Farnsworth and I would ever become good friends.

"A detective, I understand?"

"Yessir." Now I sounded like the kid at the desk.

"There's no trouble, I hope."

"Not really. I'm just trying to get a few questions answered."

"I've got Rotary early today. I'll help you if I can—if you're not going to be here long."

"I appreciate that." From inside my sport jacket, I took a photo of Richard Coburn and set it on the desk. "I just wonder if you knew this man."

"Richard Coburn."

"You knew him, then?"

"From the newspapers and television anyway. I assume you're aware he was murdered."

"Yes, I am aware of that, Mr. Farnsworth." I paused. "So other than the newspaper and the television you didn't know him?"

"Did I say that?"

"I guess not."

"I'd appreciate it if you didn't put words in my mouth, Mr. Dwyer."

"All right."

He sighed. He looked disturbed. "I don't want to drag the motel into any of this."

"I understand."

"I own fifty percent of it and my brother-in-law owns the other fifty percent. He's a lay minister in one of the local Lutheran churches. If that tells you anything."

"He wants the motel run strictly for business?"

"Exactly. He'd be happy if everybody who checked in here brought their wife and kids and if they spent the night in their rooms singing hymns."

I laughed out loud. Maybe Farnsworth here wasn't as bad as I'd judged him.

"In other words," he said, "I want everything I

say to you to remain confidential."

"I understand."

His mean eyes looked furtive momentarily. He looked around as if checking for listening devices and said, "Richard and I were drinking friends."

"I see."

"He was a hellion."

"That's what I heard."

"One night in Chicago I was told by a hooker that he took on three different women and managed to show all of them a good time."

I thought of his inability to make love to Deirdre. He must have hated her terribly.

"Did he use your place often?" I asked.

"All the time." He shook his head. He seemed caught between admiration and disgust. "It was like a beauty pageant."

"Anybody in particular?"

"Anybody he could wile up here. And Richard was a very resourceful man." He shrugged. "Of course, we kind of drifted apart the last year."

"Why's that?"

He pointed to the wide, diamond-filled ring on his wedding finger. "I got hitched again." I hadn't heard "hitched" since the Fifties. It had a quaintness about it. "And my wife didn't approve of Richard at all."

"But he came here anyway?"

"Oh, sure. I didn't stop liking him. I just stopped trying to be like him. I decided to start acting my age."

"Do you know his partner Anton?"

He smiled. "I know his partner, I know his wife Deirdre and I know his mistress Jackie. They're quite a team."

"A team?"

"Sure. Every once in a while, Richard would exasperate them to the point that they'd forget all about disliking each other and get together and beat him down. That's when he really used this place. Whenever Richard got real low, he'd start hitting on the women really hard. He liked his booze but nothing seemed to work for his self-esteem like women." He frowned. "There was only one thing I didn't approve of."

"What was that?"

He looked furtive again. "It's so sleazy I almost hate to say it. When I found out about it, I really raised hell with Richard. I told him that if he ever brought her here again, I'd personally call the law on him. Christ, this is the kind of thing men go to prison for."

"What kind of thing?"

"Underage girls."

"He was into underage girls?"

"Only one so far as I knew, but in her case one was enough." He glowered. "Mignon Anton."

I wanted to say something dramatic, but all I did was sit there and let the information make its slow inevitable way into my mind. Of course an ass-bandit such as Richard Coburn would look for the ultimate conquest—and what better a conquest than a beautiful sixteen-year-old girl? If Coburn had been in the room, I would have smashed his face in.

" Jesus Christ," I said. I thought of my own daughter and felt sick.

"Richard could get to you at times."

"Does her father know?"

"Not as far as I know."

"How long did it go on?"

"All I can tell you about is how many times he brought her here."

"All right."

"I don't think it was much longer than a month or two."

"Why do you say that?"

"Because the next time he came here—after I warned him about Mignon, that is—he brought somebody else."

"Any idea who she was?"

"Stewardess. He majored in stewardesses."

"Anybody regular after that?"

"Not that I could tell."

"How about around the time of his death?"

He thought a moment. "Nobody special. Some more stewardesses." He smiled. "Enviably enough, Richard was into quantity as well as quality. In fact, I sometimes used to think that he preferred quantity to quality."

"Did he ever get into it with anybody over a woman?"

"A jealous lover, you mean?"

I nodded.

"No, not really. A few altercations in bars over the years—Richard wasn't averse to fistfights in his younger days—but it was usually because Richard would get drunk and hit on somebody who had a date with her. Sometimes when Richard got drunk, he thought he was invincible. You know how that goes."

"But no recent altercations."

"No, I'm afraid not." He sat forward. He was suddenly confidential. "It was one of them."

"Them?"

"The three of them. Tom or Deirdre or Jackie."

"Why do you say that?"

"They had the most reason to hate him. He'd managed to screw each of them over very badly."

"How did he screw Deirdre over?"

"Hard as she likes to pretend she's this really hard bitch, there was a time when she genuinely loved Richard. He sort of forced her into her role."

"By being unfaithful?"

"Richard never tried to make any secret of it."

"I'm told he spent her money."

"Most of it."

"What about Jackie?"

He sat back in his chair and stared at the gray oblong of overcast sky in his window. "I've never been able to read Jackie, if you know what I mean. There's something unknowable about her. Almost too good to be true sometimes."

"Was Richard in love with her?"

"For a time. But then Richard was in love with all of them for a time. And with Jackie he felt an obligation. He felt she helped him through a period when he was having some sexual difficulties. I read somewhere that Casanova was impotent for long stretches in his life. Maybe it's part of the Don Juan syndrome."

"Richard told you about his problems?"

He shrugged. "Poor bastard had to talk to somebody, I suppose. He was really terrified. I suppose he thought he was being punished by God or something. He was really into a lot of guilt for things, despite the way he acted sometimes." He checked his wristwatch. "I'm sorry, Mr. Dwyer, I've got to be pushing off for Rotary. I'm head of the gifts-for-tots committee this year." He stood, frowning. "My father grew up in the Depression, but I'll tell you something—I think there are more poor people now than then. And I'm not sure there's a damn thing we can do about it. The Democrats keep trying to create new bureaucracies to take care of the problem but when you think about it we've had a poverty program since the days of FDR—and now we've got more people on the dole than ever." He put his hard hand out. "I hope I don't sound heartless."

"Not at all," I said. I smiled. "That's a paid political announcement I give myself sometimes."

"Got any answers to our dilemma, Mr. Dwyer?"

"Not a damn one, Mr. Farnsworth," I said. "Not a damn one."

18

"May I help you?"

"I'd like to see Mignon, please."

"Is this is a joke?"

"Not that I know of."

"Mignon is sixteen years old."

"I realize that."

The squat woman in the housedress and the frilly white apron and the brown sensible shoes continued to glare at me. Mignon and Tom Anton lived in an expensive condominium that looked over the river to the east and a forest to the west. I was not surprised that they employed a housekeeper, even one who apparently lived on the premises.

"My name is Jack Dwyer."

"You're a friend of the family?"

"Not exactly. I'm an investigator. I'm sure Mignon will say it's all right to show me in."

"But will Mr. Anton?"

"I don't know. Go ask him."

"That's the problem. He's not here."

"I see."

She glared at me some more and then began chewing on the inside of her cheek. "All right. I'll go speak with Mignon, but you're not to come inside. Do you understand?"

"Scout's honor."

"That's not very funny."

She probably trained nuns in her spare time.

"Right there. And not one foot inside. Do you understand?"

I nodded. She went away.

After a time, a nice-looking older couple who looked to be on their way to a holiday party came out of their door down the corridor. As they went over to the elevator, struggling across the thick carpeting, they stared at me as if they'd never seen one of me before. They continued staring, discreetly of course, until their elevator came and they were packed inside.

"Hello, Jack."

When I turned back around—I'd almost been tempted to wave at the holiday couple—Mignon stood in the doorway. In a white blouse and designer jeans and her hair in a ponytail, she looked to be fourteen.

"Our housekeeper thinks you're an escaped convict."

I smiled. "I shot four orphans on my way over here."

She smiled back. "She said it was five." She leaned over and picked something up. A Levi jacket. "Do you mind standing in the cold for a few minutes?"

"I guess not."

"I'm not supposed to smoke in the apartment."

"You shouldn't smoke at all."

"You sound like our housekeeper."

"I do, don't I?"

She crossed the threshold, closed the door quietly behind her, took my hand in hers and then led me down the corridor to double glass doors that led to a veranda. Snow was piled in white dunes on both corners of the wide stone patio. She pushed through the doors and we went outside.

"It's beautiful," I said, and it was, even though it was freezing. Sunlight made the frozen river golden and steep snowy hills covered with pine trees seemed to reach all the way to the blue sky.

"You want one?"

"No, thanks."

"Did you ever smoke?"

"Too long."

"I really like it."

"I'm refraining from giving you any speeches."

"That's nice of you."

She got a cigarette going and then walked down to the opposite end of the patio. "Sometimes I stand here and try to count the stars. Do you know that old Indian legend?"

"No."

"It says that God put man on this planet to count the number of stars in the heavens."

"And what happens if we ever count them all?"

"We die. We'll have served our purpose."

"Sounds like a fun sort of God."

She inhaled deeply. The smoke was silver coming from her lovely red lips. I kept reminding myself of how young she was.

"When my mother died, I hated God," she said. "I used to tell him that all the time."

"Do you still hate him?"

"I don't hate him, but I don't like him either."

"Is that how you felt about Richard Coburn?"

"Did I hate him, you mean?"

"Yes."

"No."

"Did you love him?"

She took another drag. Suspicion had narrowed her gaze. Inside her jacket, she shivered. "Rose—you know our housekeeper—she doesn't want me to stay out here very long. Maybe I'd better have a few more drags and go back inside."

"Somebody told me you were having an affair with him."

She didn't say anything.

"Somebody told me that you used to go to a certain motel with him frequently."

She kept quiet for a while longer and then said, "I thought we were friends, Jack."

"We are."

"Friends don't attack each other."

"I'm not attacking you. I'm trying to find out the truth."

"My tenth-grade philosophy teacher told me that truth is often an illusion."

"Then your tenth-grade philosophy teacher is full of shit."

"You're very angry, aren't you?"

"I guess I am."

"Why?"

"Because you slept with Coburn."

"Isn't that sort of my business?"

"Did he rape you?"

"No."

"Coerce you?"

"No. Richard was the seducer and I was the innocent. That's what you'd like to believe, isn't it?"

"I guess."

"I lost my virginity when I was ten. I got pregnant when I was thirteen."

I said nothing.

"The fact is, Jack, I seduced Richard."

I remained quiet.

"I've always been attracted to older men. I'm attracted to you."

"I don't think you should say any more."

"Because it spoils your image of me, doesn't it?"

I shrugged.

"Doesn't it, Jack?"

"I guess." Then I said, "Did your father know about you and Richard?"

"That's why you really came here, isn't it? To find out if Tom knew—because if he did, then he would have had a good reason to kill Richard."

"Did he know?"

She flipped her cigarette into a dune of snow and then looked up at the sky. "Isn't it wonderful when you inhale cold air into your lungs?"

"Did he know, Mignon?"

"Yes."

"Did he confront Richard?"

"Several times."

"And what happened?"

"Richard just said it was our business."

She dropped her head and turned back to me. "I don't think he killed him, Jack."

"You don't sound very sure."

"That's the only thing I couldn't handle."

"What?"

"If what I did drove Tom to—" She shook her head. "If I come over there, would you give me a hug?"

"Maybe that's not a good idea."

"I'm not playing the seductress, Jack. I just need to be—held. Don't you ever need to be held?"

She came over. She pushed her arms around me and held me tight. She put her head against my chest. "I wish you liked me, Jack."

"Don't play games here, Mignon. You know I like you but I don't approve of how you live."

"I don't either, really, but I'm not sure how else to do it."

"Try finding friends your own age, for starters. And try staying out of the Avanti."

"Tom likes to take me there."

"The hell with Tom."

She held me tighter. "Do you have any kids?"

"A boy and a girl."

"What's the girl's name?"

I told her.

"I wish I was her," she said. "I wish I was your daughter."

I kissed her forehead. "Come on, kiddo. We're both starting to freeze."

But she held so tight I couldn't move. "There's a boy," she said.

"A boy?"

"In eleventh grade."

"I see."

"He's cute but he's also kind of dorky. But I like him."

"Yeah?"

"Umm-hmm. I was even thinking of asking him to the Christmas dance."

"Why don't you?"

"Because the other girls wouldn't think he was cool enough."

"To hell with the other girls."

She laughed and pulled away from me. She took my hand again and tugged me toward the glass door. "You have such simple solutions to things, Jack," she said. "That's why I like you."

At her door I kissed her on the forehead again. She went inside, Rose standing in the doorway. Mignon looked at her and then at me and smiled sadly. I left.

19

The Ardmore Chemical Company was located a mile off the football stadium exit. It was a two-story concrete-block building that had been white-washed not too long ago. From the looks of the parking lot, Ardmore seemed to employ maybe fifty people. Judging by the age and condition of their cars, no one there seemed to be doing so well. Presumably the five-year-old Porsche belonged to the owner.

Before going inside, I sat in the Toyota reading through the page-one story about the man found dead out on Siwash Road last night. His name had been Brian Ingram, he was thirty-eight, a chemist, husband of a Sally N. Ingram, and father of two children. The body had been discovered when police responded to an anonymous phone call around eleven P.M. He had been killed by gunshot and at this time police were "considering several leads." Right.

The Ardmore lobby was small and filled with cheap furniture. After speaking to the receptionist, I sat in a wobbly armchair and looked through a three-year-old issue of *Parents* magazine. Don't laugh. It was better than the other choices—two Chamber of Commerce brochures on the splendors of our city and a numismatics magazine. At least *Parents* had photographs of pretty young mothers.

"Mr. Dwyer?"

He was early forties, potbellied behind a blue vest that matched the rest of his suit, and tired behind rimless spectacles.

I stood up. His handshake was strong but damp.

"I'm Bevins. Charles Bevins. The owner."

I felt self-conscious. Were we going to have our talk out in the reception area? The secretary pretended to be typing, but you could see that she was listening, too.

"I wondered if we could talk about Brian Ingram a little bit."

His full lips pursed. "Poor Brian. Poor Sally. Poor kids."

"I'm sorry about it."

"This city. This city." He shook his head, apparently feeling restrained from saying what he wanted to about this city. "When I was growing up here, you could go anywhere. Anywhere. And nobody would bother you."

Apparently Charles Bevins had grown up near the golf course of the city's biggest country club because other than that there were a lot of places you couldn't go back in the good old days we've all invented. Especially if you happened to be black or Hispanic.

"I wondered—"

"I'm afraid I'm very busy, Mr. Dwyer."

"Five minutes."

He glanced at his receptionist and gave her one of those tiny looks that are really code for Why is this jerk pestering me today of all days?

"Well, I have to check over a packaging machine's operation. If you don't mind tagging along, I can give you a few minutes."

"Fine."

He looked back at the receptionist again. "Sheila, hold my calls for half an hour, would you please? We'll be back in the packaging room."

Ardmore proved to be much larger than it appeared from the outside, a maze of corridors leading to various tiny offices and production departments. All the employees looked casual, slacks or jeans. You could see that some of the women had been beautiful once but had now slipped into indifference and glum age. Most of the men just looked defeated and weary in socially acceptable ways—resignation but no rage. The odor of different chemical solutions varied from department to department. We passed through a lunchroom that looked like a monument to vending machines. People were on their morning coffee break. Two or three of the women had been crying recently. You could safely assume the subject had been Brian Ingram. In a company this small, the violent death of an employee would hold the fascination of scandal. Past the lunchroom, I saw a large production facility where big nipples dispensed chemical solutions of various colors—yellow, green, amber—and various consistencies into various sizes of bottles. When filled, the bottles jiggled down a long, looping production belt that carried them through a wide opening in the east wall. It was the other side of this wall where we stopped, at a window through which you could see the jiggling chemical bottles lifted by automated steel hands and placed surely into slots inside cardboard boxes.

"Five hundred boxes an hour," Charles Bevins said. He sounded like a parent telling you that his son had just made the honor roll. "Had it installed last week." He nodded to the people loading the cardboard boxes on the start track of the assembly belt. "Someday, we won't need people for even that." He seemed pleased with this prospect—the ideal world: no people.

He watched the assembly line a few more minutes and then turned to me.

"So you want to talk about Brian."

"If we could."

"Do you mind if I ask why you want to talk about Brian?"

"I'm a private investigator, Mr. Bevins."

"I see. And why would a private investigator be involved in a case such as this?"

"I'm not sure."

"Now that's an interesting answer, Mr. Dwyer. You drive out here and bother me when I'm very busy, yet when it comes right down to it you're not sure why you want to see me."

Most of us plain folk have to eat a one-pound bag of shit a day to survive. Charles Bevins was handing me mine.

"I'm interested in his background."

"In Brian's background?"

"Yes. I'm investigating another case and his name came up.

"In what context did his name come up?"

"No particular context. His name just came up."

Bevins turned his gaze back to the assembly belt. It seemed to reassure him in some way. "You have no way of knowing this, but I'm the godfather of Brian's children."

"No, I wasn't aware of that."

"My wife is also a very good friend of Sally."

"Oh."

He turned his eyes back to me. "It's been good for our employees to see that just because I'm the president doesn't mean that I'm aloof. That's just good management technique. Don't you think?"

"It's great management technique."

He couldn't quite tell if I was mocking him or not. Neither could I.

"I always told Brian that his problems were my problems. He knew that my office door was always open."

"Ah."

"And whenever he had a problem, he'd come in and see me."

"What sort of problems did Brian have?"

His eyes narrowed. "The sort you'd expect a re-spectable, hard-working, middle-class family man to have. Making ends meet. Setting up a college fund for the girls. Finding the right retirement plan to supplement the generous one we offer here."

His tone challenged me to argue with any of

this, particularly with his characterization of his retirement plan as "generous."

"He wasn't a chaser, then?"

"I'm going to pretend you didn't say that."

"And he didn't have a drinking problem."

"No, Mr. Dwyer, and he wasn't a child molester or a transvestite, either. Just a respectable, hard-working, middle-class family man. In fact, I often used him as an example in my column."

"Your column?"

"I publish a little newsletter for my employees. You know, pictures of my family and our dog and the new house we've built and all the family things we've been up to. My wife Caroline is very active in the Junior League and the employees just love to read about all the things Caroline and her League friends do."

"I bet."

He looked me over for any signs of sarcasm again.

"In other words, Mr. Dwyer. You've been misled. Poor Brian was just what he seemed to be."

"A respectable, hard-working, middle-class family man."

"Exactly."

I put out my hand. We shook. His was pretty wet again. Maybe his wife Buffy or whatever her name was would get him some hand towels for Christmas and maybe they could do a story about that for the employee newsletter. I wondered how you got on the mailing list.

"Would you like me to see you out, Mr. Dwyer?"

"I think I can find my way."

He turned back to the automated assembly line. "Good. Then I'll just stand here and watch this." He smiled to himself. "Five hundred boxes an hour."

"That's what you said."

The faces had changed in the lunchroom. There were three new overweight women over in a corner eating from brown lunch sacks. One of them was crying pretty hard while she chomped on a cookie. The other two women on either side of her patted her shoulder as if she were a big sad dog.

In the reception area I started out the door, not paying much attention to the receptionist, when she said, "Mr. Dwyer?"

"Yes?"

"It's my lunch hour."

I turned back, not sure why she'd told me this.

"I eat at Smitty's down the street. They have wonderful roast beef sandwiches."

I still said nothing.

"I know you were asking about Brian. I—" And here she glanced around anxiously. "I'd be happy to talk to you about him."

Smitty's was a working-class restaurant where for two dollars and fifty cents you could get a decent cut of meat, mashed potatoes that were the real thing, green beans that still had a little crisp in them, and a piece of peach pie I'd have eaten two of if I'd been alone. Ordering two pieces of pie in front of somebody else is sort of like making her privy to your darkest sexual secrets. That's right, ma'm, I really enjoy making love to muskrats and I *always* have two pieces of pie.

"He was a swinger," she told me.

I glanced up from my potatoes. I was kind of mashing them up with the green beans. I really should eat alone. "Beg pardon?"

"Brian." She stared at the mess I'd made of my food.

"A swinger?" I hadn't heard that word since the days of bell-bottoms and tie-dyed T-shirts.

"Absolutely."

She'd already told me her name, which was Sheila, and how long she'd been with the company, twelve years. She was too round by half and worn-looking and given the span of her hips should not have been wearing a yellow sweater and matching skirt. She had a mole riding on her right nostril and the kind of pores that in daylight look like minor craters. I felt guilty that I could sit here and think these things about somebody who was probably a very nice woman.

"You knew that for a fact?"

The way she averted her brown eyes when I said this told me more than she'd wanted to reveal. Probably it had been at an office party, Brian Ingram's wife at home with the flu or a sick kid, and there'd been a lot of drinking, and certainly a few Americana speeches from his employer Bevins, and then—a ride home, perhaps—sex of the sort that nobody ever feels very good about afterward.

"We were friends."

"I see."

"He needed somebody to kind of, well, mother him. You know." Her voice was as bleak as her eyes.

"Right."

"He always told me everything. What happened to him on the road, things like that."

"What did he do there?"

She nodded. "He started out as a chemist but the last five years, he developed a small territory for himself and started selling our products. He liked sales much better. He hated to be in an office all day. I knitted him a special sweater for his first day on the road. That was five years ago." She looked out at the parking lot. Guys scraped their windows and swooshed snow off back windows and gave other guys pushes when back tires got stuck. It had been snowing for the past hour or so. The plate-glass window next to my elbow was freezing cold. In places the crusty window ice had started to melt from the heat inside and there were little puddles on the glass every few feet or so. "He'd listen to me and I'd listen to him. That's why we were such good friends."

"Did he seem depressed or anxious about anything lately?"

"Yes."

"Do you know why?"

"He thought maybe his wife had found out."

"Found out?"

"You know, that he had somebody on the side."

"Did he have somebody on the side?"

She thought a moment. "Not very often and not for very long. Basically, he loved his wife and girls."

"But every once in a while—"

"He was very fat as a boy."

"I see."

"So it was kind of like he had to prove it to himself."

"Prove what?"

"That women found him desirable."

"Oh."

She looked me over. "You don't seem the type. You seem very secure."

"I'm not."

"Really?"

"Uh-huh. I think I'm just as ugly and unseemly as the next guy."

She giggled. "You're funny. In a good way, I mean."

I paused. "So he was afraid his wife had found out."

"He met some old flame."

"When was this?"

"A few weeks ago."

"He told you this?"

"Sure. We had drinks several times a month. He was fun to get drunk with because he'd get so silly. He really liked to have a good time. It was very

. . . innocent." She sounded just a hair forlorn about that; and again I sensed the wound of her loneliness.

"So did it heat up again with this old flame?"

"That's the funny thing."

"What?"

"That was one of the few times he got secretive around me. Me. Imagine."

"Did you prod him at all?"

"I just asked him if anything was wrong."

"And he said what?"

"He said that he'd better not talk about it."

"But he seemed nervous?"

She looked out the window again. "Yes. I guess that'd be a fair word. Nervous."

"But he didn't give you any hint about what at all?"

"Just that maybe he was in over his head."

"He said that?"

"Those were his exact words."

"That he was in over his head?"

"Yes."

"You assumed he was talking about the woman?"

She looked at me curiously. "What else would he have been talking about?"

"I'm not sure."

"Was he in trouble?"

"Not that I know of."

"You just told me a lie," she said.

"What?"

"I'm very good at reading faces. Very good. And

I could see that you just told me a lie. Your whole body language. You were very uncomfortable."

"Oh."

"You really think he was in trouble, don't you?"

"I guess I think it was a possibility."

I sipped some coffee and stared outside at the whipping snow.

After a time, she said, "Poor Brian."

A man who was pushing the backside of a Pontiac Firebird tripped when the car pulled free. He fell face forward like a Keystone Kop.

I said, "Do you remember anything at all he said about the woman?"

"Not really."

"No name, no address, no occupation?"

"Oh. Yes. One thing. High school."

"High school?"

"They went to high school together. Is that any help?"

"That could be a great deal of help. Thank you."

"Poor Brian."

"He's probably not 'poor Brian' anymore. He probably has other considerations now."

"Heaven?"

"Something like that."

"Do you really believe in heaven?"

"I try to."

"I wish I could. I was raised Lutheran and all." She looked down at her plump white fingers. "Mr. Coleman says if there was a heaven we'd he able to prove it."

"Mr. Coleman?"

"He's the man who lives down the hall from me. Sometimes we go out and have dinner or take in a movie. I think he's gay. He sells shoe appliances. That's always sounded weird to me. 'Shoe appliances.' Doesn't it sound weird to you?"

"Shoe appliances. Very weird indeed."

"I can tell you want to go."

"Really?"

"Body language. You're squirming like a little boy in church. Not that I blame you. You want to find out about the woman he was seeing. His high school flame and all. And anyway, I'm not very good company."

"You're wonderful company."

"I'm wonderful company for people like Mr. Coleman maybe. But not for people like you and Brian."

For the first time, tears stood in her eyes. I was filled with a sense of her quiet loneliness and I wished I weren't so shallow and could ask her out despite the fact that she'd elicit no whistles in singles bars.

I reached out and covered her hand in mine. She cried even more but silently, just big wet silver tears, and then she put her other hand over mine and said, "I really did love him."

"I know."

She sort of laughed then. "I'll bet you're embarrassed sitting here with me crying. The middle of the day in a public place."

"I'm not embarrassed at all."

"Whoever gets you is a lucky woman," she said.

I smiled. "She might not agree with that."

"It's all right if you go, Mr. Dwyer. I've still got twenty minutes so I wouldn't mind just relaxing." She tamped her purse. "Anyway, it's time for one of my two cigarettes."

"Two a day, huh?"

"It's been that way for twenty years. Brian always laughed about it. Said I should just give them up." She stared up at me and daubed at a single silver tear with the tip of a plump finger. "But sometimes that's all the pleasure we get. Just a little bit."

I leaned over and kissed her on the forehead. "Take care of yourself." I picked up the check to pay it on my way out.

She patted my hand. When I went outside and scraped off the window, I could see her watching. I waved goodbye. She waved goodbye back.

20

At the office I went through three stacks of pink phone slips, making two piles of them, one that needed to be dealt with right away, one that could be put off until the real boss returned.

By midafternoon, I had addressed the worst of the problems and was just starting to dial Brian Ingram's number when the intercom announced that it was a phone call for me.

"Who is it?" I asked Bobby Lee.

"He wouldn't say. He don't sound real polished, if you know what I mean."

I picked up the receiver. "Dwyer."

"I seen you at St. Mark's. You didn't see me, though."

"All right."

"When you was here the other day."

"Right."

"Talking to Miss—"

"I remember the day, my friend. How can I help you?"

"I, uh, have some information you might be interested in."

"Oh?"

"Uh-huh. But I couldn't give it to you free."

"Why not?"

"You don't think I need money? I ain't stayin' in

St. Mark's all my life."

"I guess that makes sense. How much money are we talking about?"

"Couple hundred."

"That could be done."

"And somethin' else, too."

"All right."

"You don't say nothin' to Miss Daily."

"Got it."

Hesitation. "So you'll pay me the two hundred?"

"If I like what I see."

"Seven o'clock on the corner of St. Mark's. My name's Conroy."

"Conroy."

"Seven."

"Right."

"And two hundred."

"Two hundred. Right."

From three o'clock till five o'clock I tried Brian Ingram's house fifteen times. Patience is not one of my primary virtues. No answer. A married woman suddenly widowed would have many friends to turn to and many duties to carry out, not least among them choosing a funeral parlor, casket, and church, at which tasks Mrs. Ingram was probably busy right now.

After work, I went back to my room to see how my new friend the kitty was doing. She had apparently gotten used to the place, sitting on a cushion on the wooden rocker right in front of the TV set, as if waiting for me to come home and turn the thing on.

I stirred the sand in her litter box, poured out fresh milk and dry food into adjoining bowls, and then went into the john for a quick shower. Tonight I wore my gray tweed suit, knowing that somehow I'd end up at the Avanti. Maybe I was becoming a swell and didn't even know it.

I tried the Ingram woman again but again no answer. Before leaving, I sat on the cushion in the rocker with the kitty in my lap. The front room was dark except for street light against the frosted windowpane. Wind came howling, sounding lonely, and from downstairs faintly you could hear Bing Crosby singing "White Christmas" on the radio. I wondered what my kids were doing. I wondered what Donna was doing. I stroked the kitty. She climbed up the front of my suit and nuzzled me with her tiny wet pink nose and then licked me a few times idly on the jaw with her little sandpaper tongue. I gave her a soft hug—I could feel her ribs and that almost scared me she was so delicate—and then the phone rang. I set the kitty down carefully and she cried as if she'd been deserted and, hell, I did feel as if I'd deserted her and then I got the phone.

"Jack?"

"Yes."

"This is Gwen Daily. You were at St. Mark's—"

"Sure, Gwen."

"Something's happened."

"Oh?"

"Did you by any chance talk to a man named Albert Conroy tonight?"

I thought about it and decided to tell her. "I talked to a Conroy. I'm not sure his first name was Albert. Why?"

"He's in the hospital."

"What happened?"

"I'm not sure, but it appears that somebody struck him on the head with something heavy."

"He's dead?"

"No, but he has a very bad concussion."

"Can he tell the police who struck him?"

"He won't. He's very reticent about everything."

"I guess I'm not sure why you called me."

"Because on his bed I found a piece of paper with your name and number on it."

"I see."

"That's all you have to say?"

The kitty stood on the cushion looking at me and crying her tiny cry. In the silver frosted light, she looked even more frail.

"You sound as if I hit him, Gwen."

"No, I'm not accusing you of that, but I would like to know what the hell's going on. I'm not big on subterfuge, Jack."

"He called me."

"Conroy called you? For what?"

"He wanted to sell me a piece of information."

"Information about what?"

"I'm not sure."

"What did you tell him?"

"I agreed to meet him on the corner at seven o'clock."

"This really irritates me, Jack."

"I figured it would."

"I'm in charge here. The least you could have done was inform me about the call."

"I apologize."

"It really makes me very angry."

I didn't say anything for a time, just listened to the kitty mewl.

"I'm sorry I got so angry."

"That's all right," I said. "I would have been angry, too." I laughed. "Would now be a good time to ask you a favor?"

"What kind of favor?"

"I'd like to look through his belongings."

"Conroy's?"

"Right."

"What for?"

"I'm not sure. Maybe I'll stumble across what he wanted to sell me."

"You'd recognize it?"

"Maybe. I assume it has to do with Coburn's murder."

"What would Conroy know about that?"

"That's what I'd like to find out."

Pause. "You want to come over, then?"

"I'd appreciate it."

"Right away?"

"Soon as I can get there."

Now she laughed. "I can't believe I'm letting you do this after you were such a shit to me. You really owed me a call about Conroy."

"I know."

"I must really like men who treat me badly. You know?"

"Well," I said, "we all have to like somebody."

Halfway to St. Mark's, I pulled into a drive-up phone, deposited a quarter, and on the second ring got a female voice that I had every reason to believe was Mrs. Brian Ingram's.

"Yes?"

"Are you Mrs. Ingram?"

"Yes."

"First of all I want to apologize, Mrs. Ingram. I know this is a bad time to call."

"Who is this, please?"

"My name is Jack Dwyer. I'm a private investigator. There's no reason you should know me."

"What is it you'd like? Oh—just a minute, Mr. Dwyer." In the background, I heard her giving two youngsters directions about lighting the Christmas tree, telling them which plugs went where. When she came back, she said, "The girls insist that they light the tree themselves. That's part of the fun, I suppose." She sounded lovely and exhausted. I wanted to give her the same sort of hug I'd given the kitty earlier this evening. "May I ask you a question, Mr. Dwyer?"

"Of course."

"Do you know anything about my husband's death?"

"If you're asking me who killed him, Mrs. Ingram, I'm afraid I don't have any idea."

"I guess I've learned two things in the past twenty-four hours."

"What things, Mrs. Ingram?"

"That ordinary, middle-class people like Brian really do get murdered. And now I've learned that private investigators exist outside of TV programs." She cupped the phone. I heard her say, "It looks beautiful, girls," and then to me, "How may I help you, Mr. Dwyer?"

"I would like to come over and talk to you for a while."

"Tonight?"

"I'm afraid it should be tonight."

"You sound very urgent about something."

"I'm working on something that may or may not have some bearing on your husband's death, Mrs. Ingram."

"His parents aren't dealing with it well at all. His father had a stroke last spring and his mother has rheumatoid arthritis."

"I'm sorry."

"The doctor gave his father a sedative last night and it made his whole mouth break out."

I sighed. You don't die alone; in very real ways, you take many others with you.

"I'm sorry to have to ask you this."

"The house is a mess."

"That's fine."

"When were you thinking of coming over?"

"How does an hour and a half sound?"

"Could you make it two hours?"

"All right."

"I can get the girls to bed and make a pot of tea. Do you like tea, Mr. Dwyer?"

"Very much. Especially on cold winter nights."

"You'll have some identification?"

"I'll do better than that, Mrs. Ingram."

"Oh?"

"I'll give you a phone number to call. It belongs to a man named Edelman who's a detective on the city police force. He'll vouch for me."

"That's very courteous of you, Mr. Dwyer."

I gave her the number and drove over to St. Mark's.

21

The aromas of steam-table food hung on in the air. In a large barren room perhaps two dozen men sat on the floor watching three different television sets, two of which were tuned to different channels. In one small cubicle a counselor of some kind tried to calm down a man who was deeply aggrieved. In a lounge area two men sat at opposite ends of a sofa smoking cigarettes and disregarding each other utterly. One of the men was carrying on a conversation with himself; he went so far as to laugh sharply at certain of his own remarks. I suspected this was all pretty much a typical night for St. Mark's.

Gwen Daily was in her office. She was working her way through a stack of forms. She was also sitting directly beneath the NO SMOKING PLEASE sign and inhaling deeply of a filter cigarette.

The floorboards squeaked as I reached the threshold. She looked up. "Fast trip."

"Light traffic."

She shook her head. "I just got a call from the hospital about Conroy. They expect him to be in there for two weeks."

"But he still won't talk about who did it?"

"He's scared." She wore a bulky blue sweater and looked almost like a sorority girl. She bit at one of her fingernails and said, "Whether we like to admit it or not, there are some real predators in this place. Conroy obviously believes that whoever did this to him can do it to him again."

"So obviously he did find something."

"Obviously." She stubbed out her cigarette and stood up. She wore snug jeans. Her hips and her bottom looked wonderful. She was aware of my glimpse and said, "I wish my new friend was as appreciative as you."

"That'll teach you to go out with blind guys."

"Chivalrous," she said, and poked me in the ribs. "I like that."

I followed her out of the office and down the corridor to the doors leading to the sleeping area.

As she put her hand on the knob, she said, "Do you have any idea what you're looking for?"

"No. Do you?"

"Uh-uh."

"We make a great team."

The men not watching television or sitting in the lounge were already in their beds for the night. They would be of various kinds—men so hassled by the streets and the cold weather that they didn't want to leave the snugness of their beds; men afraid of other human beings, even those in the shelter; men given to the kind of brooding that teetered on madness, obsession, I suppose—the inability to let go. I could tell you a few things about that myself.

They watched us as we worked our way up the aisle between the cots and the air mattresses. It was like a big boot-camp barracks, but untidy and slightly sour-smelling, and the men who watched you weren't farm kids with dreams of booze and hookers dancing in their heads but fearful old men of various ages long past hope or any real solace.

One of them, who was bent over straightening up his bedclothes, bumped me when I passed him. "Sumbitch," he said, jerking up to glare at me. He said this without benefit of teeth, not even false ones.

"Calm down, Peter," Gwen Daily said. She reached out and touched him near an open sore on the tip of his elbow. "And I've told you, you go down the street to the infirmary and have them take care of that okay?"

But he was still glaring at me, the way drunks do in taverns when they're about ready to square off.

"Peter. Do you hear me?"

She was half-shouting at him.

"Peter. Do you hear me?"

She poked him in the elbow. For a scrawny, bent old fart his rage had a certain crazed majesty and I knew if I punched him hard he'd withstand it and punch me right back.

"You lie down, Peter. And right now, do you hear me?"

Something got through to him finally because the glazed glare left his gaze. He blinked and said, "Sumbitch."

"You lie down there, Peter. Do you hear me?"

"Yes'm," he said, all of a sudden the docile boy.

We went on down the aisle to Conroy's bed.

"Schizophrenic," she said. "In and out of the mental hospital, but they won't keep him long enough to do him any good." I saw then, abruptly, like an insight in a novel, how much she cared for this job. Nothing dramatic, but the real thing, and I liked the hell out of her just then and gave her a little hug.

"You might have made a good nun after all, Daily, you know that?" I said.

She shook her head. "I just feel so sorry for most of them. And there's almost nothing I can do."

Conroy's cot was near the back, in the shadows, flush against a brick wall that felt like forty below to the touch.

There was nothing remarkable about it. Like most of the cots, it was swaybacked from too many bodies for too many years. The bedclothes—stained but clean sheets, pillows greasy from hair oil, and prison-rough woolen blanket—were in tangles. A single white work sock dangled off the paint-chipped metal tubing that passed for a headboard. On the wall above the board was taped—black electrical tape; nothing fancy here—a fading photograph of a young man in an Army uniform. A private. The young man was alone, smoking a cigarette in the fashion of James Dean, and leaning against a 1954 Ford Fairlane. You wondered what sad trail had led Conroy from that Fairlane to this homeless shelter these long and inexplicable years later.

"He was a handsome man," Gwen Daily said.

"Not anymore, I take it?"

She traced a line with a bitten fingernail down her cheek. "Knife scar. I think it happened in prison. Armed robbery, I think the charge was." She shrugged. "Today he just drifts."

I saw it sticking out from beneath his bed. Just a corner of it.

"He's got some kind of suitcase down there," I said. "I'll need your permission to check it out."

"That's why we're here. Be my guest."

I got down on my hands and knees and pulled the suitcase out. It was cardboard and had been taped over and over, almost neurotically, with the same black electrical tape that fastened Conroy's photograph to the wall. At the latches, the tape had been cut so the two halves could be opened. I got it up on the bed and got it open and looked inside.

Mostly it was underwear stained yellow and brown in the appropriate places but bleach-washed so it could be worn again and again. There were two wrinkled *Hustler* women of their respective months, really lewd stuff that brought a prim grimace to Gwen Daily's tiny Catholic-girl mouth, and a half-filled bottle of Aqua Velva green and a cheap hairbrush and comb set and a blue necktie twenty years old but with a kind of obstinate dignity, the kind farmers wear around sunburned necks to bury their dead.

Under the underwear, I found the photograph. At first I recognized neither person. I just stared at it. It was black and white and had been folded in the middle for a long time because some of the coating had become minuscule flakes. It showed two men, one maybe forty, the other maybe twenty, standing in front of a river. The older man had his arm around the younger man. You could see they were both straining to smile at the instructions of the person taking the picture. There was nothing notable about the way they were dressed—clean casual clothes neither expensive nor shoddy. It was the same with their haircuts and their demeanor. Nothing special. Despite the fact that there was no particular resemblance between the two, you sensed that they were father and son.

"May I see?"

I handed her the photo.

She picked the older man off right away. "It's Karl."

"Is he the priest? The one always quoting the Bible?"

"Yes." She stared at the photo again and shook her head. "It really is Karl."

"Have you recognized the boy yet?"

"No."

"Look closely. And put forty pounds on him."

"My God."

"Exactly."

"But it can't be."

"It is."

"But Karl and Richard—"

"Karl must be Richard's father," I said. Then, "Is Karl here?"

"I saw him earlier."

"You want to help me round him up?"

"Of course." She looked at the photo again. "But why would Conroy have this?"

"I suppose he thought the police would be interested in it. Which would make it worth money to somebody—namely me. I'm sure he took it from Karl and I'm sure it was Karl who beat him up. And now I can see why Conroy won't talk. Karl is a pretty spooky guy."

"Karl and Richard," she said again, amazed.

I was amazed, too. I just managed to hide it better.

There were corners and rooms and closets and hideouts in the old church nobody but Gwen Daily could possibly know about. We went into places that were dark, we went into places that were damp, we went into places that were freezing—anywhere Karl might be hiding. He would have to consider the possibility that Conroy would lose his fear and start talking to the police and that the police in turn would come for him. Being Richard Coburn's father didn't necessarily make him a murder suspect but it at least made him suspicious, particularly since he'd been caught a few times hanging around the back door of the restaurant.

We didn't find him.

We spent an hour—I called Brian Ingram's wife and told her I'd been detained—and we didn't find him at all.

We ended up back in Gwen's office.

"My God, how it must have hurt Richard."

"His father being a derelict?"

"Yes. His pride. If any of his society friends had ever found out—"

"Karl may have killed him."

"But why?"

"Lots of reasons. Maybe Karl threatened to expose Richard in some way. From my two encounters with him, Karl didn't strike me as particularly stable. In fact, he struck me as insane."

She sighed. "He's another one who belongs in a mental hospital but they won't take him, of course. 'Not enough funds for people like him.' They'll wait till he kills somebody and—" Then she caught herself. "He really could have killed Richard, couldn't he?"

"Yes."

"Should we call the police?"

"Not yet. See if he comes back tonight. If he does, leave a message with my answering service. I'll call my beep and come over right away."

"You have a beeper?"

"Yup."

"Somehow I can't imagine you with a beeper."

"I have a beeper and I wear Hush Puppies sometimes. Brown ones."

She laughed. "Now, that I'll never believe." She had the photograph spread out on the desk before her. "I'm trembling." The laughter was long gone now. "Poor Richard," she said.

"That's encouraging," I said.

"What?"

"Maybe he wasn't just another one of your masochistic affairs."

"Really?"

"Maybe you loved him."

"And that should make me feel better?"

"Sure," I said, sensing how she felt now. "Isn't it better to know that you can truly love somebody instead of just having some neurotic hankering for him?"

She laughed again but this time the drabness of it fit the drabness of her office. " 'Neurotic hankering,' " she said. "Now there's a depressing description."

Five minutes later, I was in my Toyota, fishtailing through newly fallen snow, heading out the expressway to Brian Ingram's house.

22

The Ingram house was an older home in a hilly neighborhood that Dutch elm disease had apparently passed by. Easy to imagine this place in the Forties, just after the war, Hudsons and Kaisers and Henry J's pulling into the snug driveways, husbands home from office or plant for a cozy night by fire and radio.

Even with the funeral wreath on the door, the two-story white frame house seemed warm and inviting, the light in the windows laying a golden strip across the snow.

Brian Ingram's widow was a pleasant-looking if slightly plump woman in a brown V-neck sweater and wheat-colored jeans. "Won't you come in, Mr. Dwyer?"

"Thank you."

The front room in which we stood was simple but elegant, nappy wine-colored carpeting covering the floor, a fieldstone fireplace on the east wall and built-in bookcases on the west wall. A formidable Christmas tree stood in the corner nearest the closet, its lights winking on and off and covering the sprawling array of gifts with red and blue and green light. You could see where youngsters had draped silver tinsel over the branches—over-draped, really, in knots and clumps. Little hands, big ambitions. They'd probably been very proud of their work.

"Would you care for some tea, Mr. Dwyer?"

"That would be nice."

She pointed to a sofa. I slipped my shoes off and went over and sat on the couch.

She was back in two minutes. The tea was sweet and fine. She sat across the room from me in a leather recliner. "I take it you never met Brian."

"No, I didn't." I smiled. "I'm afraid I don't know your name."

"I'm sorry. It's Sally."

"Sally. Mine's Jack."

She nodded. "He worked very hard."

"He was a chemist at one time, right?"

"Correct."

"But he gave it up."

"There was more money in sales. And besides, Brian was"—she chose her word carefully—"restless. Not all the time but sometimes."

"Restless." I met her eyes.

"I didn't mean to make it sound as if it were a problem. It's just that some men are and some men—well, some men aren't."

"His employer said that Brian was an exemplary family man." I kept thinking about Sheila's notion that Brian feared his wife knew about his current affair.

"You met Mr. Bevins, then?"

I nodded.

She smiled. "He's stuffy, I know, but he means

well and he's always been very kind to Brian and me and the girls."

"He said Brian was a model employee and a model parent." The smile again—quick, sweet, endearing. I thought again of the Forties just after the war. Not only did this house recall that era, so did she. She would be defined by shopping and baking and cleaning and she would not mind it so much at all. I'd never found such women particularly appealing—I love stubborn and independent women—but meeting a Sally Ingram every once in a while is nice, sort of like enjoying an afternoon with an old Irene Dunne movie.

"I'd like to know about the last few weeks of his life," I said.

"I'm not sure what you mean." She sounded without guile or even suspicion.

"Did he behave any differently than usual?"

She thought for a time. "Not really."

"Did you notice any mood swings?"

She laughed. "With Brian, you noticed mood swings every half-hour or so."

I was about to ask another question when a small voice said, "Mommy, is that Daddy?"

On the stairway landing stood a tiny blond girl in pink pajamas complete with feet and a tiny white bunny tail. She rubbed one eye with a sweet little fist.

"No, honey, it's not Daddy. It's Mr. Dwyer."

"Who's Mr. Dwyer?"

"Just a friend of mine."

"Does he know where Daddy went?"

Sally Ingram looked across the room to me then back to the girl. "Would you like to come down and have a hug?"

"Yes, please."

"Come on then, honey."

The little girl, who was at most three, came cautiously down the steps, as if at any moment she might tumble from them into a rocky, roaring river wherein dragons dwelt. There was probably a wicked witch in there somewhere, too.

After examining me quickly, she trundled over to her mother, threw her little arms around Sally's neck, and then indulged in a long and reverent hug. As they embraced, I saw Sally's eyes close in sorrow and yearning, and saw her knuckles go white from holding her daughter so tight.

"Do you have to go to the bathroom?" Sally asked when the little girl pulled back.

"I already went."

"Good. Then say good night to Mr. Dwyer and go back to bed, honey." Sally pointed her in my direction and said, "This, by the way, is Lisa."

"Hello, Lisa."

Lisa, shy, dropped her head and stared at her pink bunny feet.

"Say good night to Mr. Dwyer."

Lisa glanced up at me again furtively and said, "G'night."

"Good night, honey."

"Now, scoot," Sally said, patting Lisa on the bottom.

Lisa, her thumb tucked comfortably in the corner of her mouth, walked by me as if staring in a department store window.

The steps up were tougher to climb than the steps down. She took very long, very careful steps and a few times I had the terrifying sensation that she was going to fall over backward. This brought back all the horrors I'd gone through when my own kids had been her age. I'd been overprotective and probably hadn't done either of them a damn bit of good.

"What a cutie," I said.

"Thank you. So's her sister Jean."

"Jean's older?"

"By two years." She said then, "I thought of two things."

"About your husband?"

"Ummm." She paused. "I want you to catch whoever killed him." She set her teacup down carefully on the end table and then stared at me. "I never thought of myself as a vengeful person. But the last few days——" She sighed. "Maybe it's what I'm drawing my strength from. Knowing that someday the person who killed him will be punished." She smiled sadly. "I keep trying to cry. But I just keep getting angry."

"You should be angry."

She said, "He did something at the lab late one night."

"I'm not sure I follow you."

"The lab has a distinctive smell. When he was

working full time as a chemist, I always said I knew when he got home because I could smell him."

"I see."

"One night a few weeks ago he got home very late. I had been asleep, but I woke up when he slipped into bed. At first I thought he might have been drinking heavily, but then I realized that the smell wasn't alcohol. It was the lab—whatever odors he always picked up there."

"Did he tell you what he was doing in the lab?"

"No."

"Did you ask him?"

"Yes."

"What did he say?"

She smiled. "When Brian didn't want to talk about something, he could change the subject so quickly you didn't even notice he was doing it."

"He changed the subject?"

She shrugged. "He wasn't always a communicative man."

"Did you smell the lab on him anymore?"

"Not after that one night."

"And you didn't notice any lasting shifts in his moods?"

"Not in his moods, no. But he got . . . sentimental. Even with the girls, he was never particularly sentimental. I knew that he loved them and loved me for that matter but he was never demonstrative and he was never sentimental the way some men are."

I thought of all the affairs he'd had according to Sheila.

"He started spending a lot of time in the den," Sally Ingram went on. "Looking at his senior yearbook."

"College?"

"High school."

"Did he say why?"

"Not Brian."

"Did you have any guess as to why?"

"No. I was just . . . shocked. He wouldn't even go to his last reunion. He said he hated those things, how everybody stood around and boasted all the time. But then all of a sudden he's spending hours poring over his high school stuff. It didn't make any sense."

"Do you suppose I could borrow the yearbook?"

She looked at me for a time. "You know things you're not telling me, don't you?"

"A few things, I suppose."

"Maybe it's just as well I don't know them."

It was a question. I didn't want to answer because to tell her what I knew would only hurt her.

"Please be very careful with it. I'll want to keep all of his things."

"Of course."

"I wish I could cry."

"You will."

"I almost feel guilty."

"After my father died fifteen years ago, I couldn't cry either," I said. "Everybody in my family took turns breaking down for a little while and really facing their grief. Except me. It went on for a month like that. Then one day I stopped over to see how my mother was doing and I sat in my father's favorite chair and I just started sobbing. When I looked back on it, I saw that various circumstances had forced me to be strong, and hold back, so I could help other people." I nodded to the girls upstairs. "You've got to be strong for them. Right now you're just not allowing yourself the luxury of grief."

"The anger feels good, though. I'm almost ashamed of myself. I really want to get the person who killed him."

I stood up. "I'm going to try, Sally. I'm going to try."

After going to get the blue and gray stiff-backed yearbook, Sally walked me to the door. I almost didn't want to leave. I wondered what it would be like to sit on the couch in the darkness with the Christmas tree all lit up and a woman like Sally under my arm. Whatever else Brian Ingram might or might not have been, he struck me as a foolish man. You didn't find Sallys very often; nor Lisas nor Jeans, either.

"I'm sorry it's so cold," she said when she opened the door for me.

I touched her shoulder. "Yes, and I'm holding you personally responsible for this weather, too."

She laughed. "God, I feel so guilty when I laugh. It's not appropriate."

"Who says it's not appropriate?"

"I don't know," she said. "It sounds like something somebody must have said."

"Nobody important."

Now I was on the porch, in the wind and the night, leaving the womb of her place.

"Good night," she said, and waved in a girlish way that looked even sweeter with the Christmas tree in the background.

23

They were shivering in the snow outside the Avanti, maybe two dozen of them, arrogant and pretty and young, pushing to get inside, their laughter high and boozy. Apparently the Avanti was so busy tonight, even the privileged had to wait outside for a few moments.

Away from the blazing light of the doorway and the cigar-store Indian of the doorman, you could see the street people, the eternal ragged ponderous zombies staring with unimaginable thoughts at the privileged young. A crone giggled madly; a shambling derelict tilted a paper-sacked wine bottle to his lips, his body giving an ecstatic jerk of pleasure.

I pushed inside. I pushed too hard and one of the pretty young men pushed back suddenly, looking as if he were about to swing on me. I grabbed him by the throat and slammed him against the door frame. The back of his head made a thwocking sound as it collided with the wood. His eyes glazed a moment. I stared at him, furious. Then I saw that he could have been my son and I said, "Jesus Christ, are you all right?" He looked more surprised by my words than he had by my action. "I apologize, kid. I'm sorry. All right?"

"Who the fuck is this guy anyway?" his girlfriend

snapped, and I didn't blame her, though the "fuck" spoiled her upper-class princess look.

"I'm just a jerk," I said to her.

"No shit," she said back.

I left them there in the snow, with their breath silver, and the gruff doorman pretending he was sorry he hadn't gotten a poke at me.

The maitre d' started toward me but decided to leave me alone. Apparently I was wearing one of those looks. Like a sixth-grade snitch, he walked over to the two bouncers—Ken was absent to-night—and whispered about me. I beat the guy into the bar and lost myself among the crowd.

I took two drinks quick, scotches, and was about to embark on a third when a familiar voice said, "You look like I feel."

I turned to find Deirdre Coburn standing next to me. She wore a simple but expensive black dress. She looked beautiful in her arch and slightly wan way. "I'm sorry I was such a bitch yesterday."

"It's what you people do—you and Tom Anton and your husband."

"Be bitchy?"

"Or push people around. The ruling elite."

"You sound bitter."

"Just weary of you all. And weary of this place."

She moved in closer. Her arm brushed mine. Curiously, I wanted her then, just quick, loveless, lonely sex in a back room somewhere. She saw it on me. "You and I could get together, Dwyer."

"Yeah, but I'd hate myself in the morning."

"Maybe I'm not as bad as you think."

I sighed. "You have your troubles, Deirdre. I can't judge you. But you don't give a damn what you do to other people—letting Earle Tomkins spend the night in jail and worrying his mother all to hell wasn't exactly a charitable act."

She said, quite seriously, "When he got home, I sent him over a check for a thousand dollars."

I stared at her a long moment and then I laughed and pulled her into me and gave her a friendly kiss on the mouth. "You're crazy and you don't even know it, Deirdre. You didn't owe him a thousand dollars. You owed him an apology."

I saw Jackie then and I set my drink down and started over for her. She was just leaving the dance floor with a portly man who looked as if he had devoted his life to selling life insurance.

I caught her by a slender wrist and moved her back to the dance floor just as the band began to play "Laura."

"I don't know if my feet are ready for another round just yet," she said.

"You look nice," I said, starting the box step.

"Thank you."

"Blue chiffon?"

"Richard gave it to me for my birthday."

"Very nice."

Something changed in her eyes. "Let's not talk about Richard." She held me more tightly. In the darkness, we danced for half the song without saying anything at all. I thought of being at a prom again.

"What did Brian Ingram find out for you?"

She kept her head tight to my shoulder. "What?"

"You gave him something, and being a chemist, he checked it out for you."

She leaned back so she could stare at me. "I don't know what you're talking about."

"Sure you do."

"I don't even know a Brian Ingram."

"You're standing right next to him in your high school yearbook."

"You sonofabitch."

We danced some more. Once I stepped on her foot but this time she didn't make any joke about it.

I said, "Something was going on at the restaurant. Whatever it was, Brian confirmed it in his laboratory. It was something that could ruin the Avanti—and that's why you killed Coburn. You decided he'd never be strong enough for you. He was sick of all his rich friends and you were afraid you would lose your investment."

She said, quite simply, "I was tired of him anyway. He was a boy. I wanted a man. You know?"

She held me again and we danced as the band segued into "Dancing in the Dark."

After a time, she said, "What are they going to do to me?"

"Take you downtown and read you your rights and see that you get a lawyer."

"I'm scared, Dwyer."

"I'm sorry."

"Do you hate me?"

"No."

"But you don't like any of us here much, do you?"

"I guess not."

"Maybe you don't understand us."

"Maybe."

"Maybe we're not as bad as we seem."

"Maybe not."

"You're being very fucking sanctimonious."

"I don't mean to be. Believe me, I don't have anything to be sanctimonious about. I'm not much in the way of being a human being, either."

"Could we dance some more and not talk?"

"Sure."

So I held her tight again and we danced the next dance and she pressed hard against me, her soft round breasts tender and white in her low-cut gown, then she said she'd like a drink before I phoned the police. I got her a drink and we sat at a cozy table and she looked gorgeous in her fleshy way and then she cried and then she giggled and then she said that her parents were going to be very embarrassed when they heard their little girl's name on television, and then Tom Anton came over looking concerned but I waved him away and then I asked her to tell me why she had to kill Brian Ingram too and she said that he'd put together that she'd killed Richard and then Brian had gotten scared and wanted out. "He really wasn't much of a man," she said, shaking her head. Then she started crying again and I got more booze into her and held her hand for a long, long time.

Finally, she told me about it, all of it, what Richard Coburn and the chef who'd quit had known about, and what Brian Ingram had confirmed in his lab.

I got up and phoned the cops and then I phoned Gwen Daily at St. Mark's and then I figured out where I might find the man I was looking for.

24

In the soft blue night, in the pale gold moonlight, in the quiet cul-de-sac where it had lain so long unused, you could hear the ghosts of the deserted factory—the whistle announcing the changing shifts, the men's safety shoes clanking up and down the steel stairs, the lunchroom alive with talk of the Cubs and Marciano and Ali, the parking lot where working-class housewives waited in new Chevrolets and Fords and the occasional Pontiac for their men. How full of promise it had been after World War II, this factory, in those giddy days when everything seemed possible—a nice tract home, shiny fine appliances, Friday nights out at a steak house, bowling with the boys on Thursday nights, even a college fund via the union for the kids.

Now, in the moonlight, it lay silent like a great rusted artifact of some alien species gone off to another world.

I stood at the bottom of the stairs that ran up the west side of the place. It was here Richard Coburn's father had crouched the other night, looking at the place with a familiarity that meant he probably came here often.

I went up ten steps to the first landing and tried the door: locked. I went up ten more steps to the

second landing and tried the next knob: locked.
On the thirtieth step, on the third landing, the knob
yielded. I opened the door on a wide, shadowy floor
that smelled of engine oil and dust and cold. Moonlight fell pale through smashed and grimy windows.
From my pocket, I took my flashlight and began
shining it around. In ten minutes I had covered the
entire floor without finding anything other than
giant turbines that had been allowed to remain here,
rusting and providing hidey-holes for rats that
chittered now at my passing.

I went down to the second floor on a set of creak-
ing interior stairs. I had just shone my light into a
corner piled high with grease-stained cardboard
boxes when a voice behind me said, "I am the bread
of life; he who comes to me shall not hunger."

Spinning around, more startled and afraid than
I cared to admit, my light picked him out in relief
against a massive gray turbine that almost reached
the murky ceiling.

He looked no less mad tonight—the bald head
knobby, the cheeks gaunt, the eyes nearly phospho-
rescent under the shelf of his brow—though he at
least wore an overcoat tonight, a shabby piece of
threadbare fabric that hung on him scarecrow-fash-
ion.

He stood pinned in my light and said, "He who
eats my flesh and drinks my blood abides in me,
and I in him."

"I'd like to help you," I said.

If he understood my words, he did not let on.

I said, "Smiley died, didn't he?"

At the name Smiley, recognition flickered in his eyes. He backed up a little as if he might cut and run.

I moved forward a step, slowly, slowly. "A few days ago, Gwen Daily at the shelter told me that the bouncers at the Avanti had beaten up a friend of yours named Smiley and that Smiley had probably gone off on a bender but nobody had seen him since."

He said, there in the gloom, in the circle of flashlight beam, "As the living Father sent me, and I live because of the Father, so he who eats of me will live because of me."

"He came here, didn't he, Smiley I mean?"

Nothing.

"He came here and died from the beating and the cold and when you found him, you got very angry, didn't you?" Still he said nothing. I said, "I'm not your enemy, old man."

"Smiley," he said. "Died."

Speaking ordinary words, instead of Bible quotations, he sounded slow, almost retarded.

"Smiley was dead and you blamed your son Richard and that's why you started doing it, wasn't it?"

"Smiley," he said. "Dead."

He looked left and right again, giving the impression that he was about to bolt.

"That's why you started sneaking into the restaurant, wasn't it? You'd cut off pieces of Smiley and then put them into the goulash and you thought nobody would know. It would be your secret from your son and from the rich people who despised the homeless like you and Smiley."

He said, "On the night he was betrayed, Jesus took bread and broke it, and said, 'This is my body.' "

"Communion," I said.

"Communion," he said. "Smiley."

That's what they'd all been afraid of—Richard had figured it out and so had Brian Ingram in his lab and he'd told Jackie. Eating human flesh at a fashionable restaurant was likely to put the restaurant out of business.

And then he ran.

He was much faster than I would have thought. In seconds, he was beyond the range of my flashlight, running in the shadows, his slapping shoes echoing in the darkness, little sobs exploding from him as he moved. Then the texture of the sounds changed—he was on metal stairs suddenly, clanging down a floor into the gloom below. I followed, pulling my .38, shouting for him to stop. I wanted to get him help of some kind; at this point, nearly any kind would do.

When I reached the first floor, I realized I'd lost him.

I tried left, I tried right. Nothing. I went down a corridor of office doors, shining my light in each room but finding nothing. I found a conference room filled with cobwebs and a walk-in closet. But nothing; nothing. I went all the way up front, to the large double doors through which the workers had entered, shining my light in every corner and cranny but he was gone. All I could figure was that he knew a quick and secret way out of here.

I went back to the center of the floor, where the skeletal remains of an assembly line ran like latticework across the middle of a vast room. In the dusty silence then, I heard him crying. All I could liken the sound to was that of a dying animal; those guttural, frightened sounds a kitten or a puppy make in your lap there at the last of their little lives.

I found him in a room stacked high with shipping crates. At first I couldn't see him, only hear him.

When I shone my light, it rested on the blue and somewhat bloated face of a derelict who had obviously been dead for some time. Smiley. But the coldness of the building had preserved him pretty well. He wore a red and black checkered hunting jacket and filthy brown trousers and a blue 7-Eleven cap. On a dead man, the cap looked funny, endearing in some stupid human way, and I almost smiled. The jacket was open and shot up the right sleeve all the way to the biceps. He had taken the flesh from the stomach and arms. Raw knife-cut gouges lay in the human meat, bloody holes ripped into the flesh. He had been smart enough to cut the meat up into small pieces so nobody could be sure what they were eating.

But a few customers had complained to Coburn

and the chef and when they looked into things, they'd learned the truth.

"Come on, old man," I said, reaching down to take his elbow. "Why don't we go back to the shelter and talk to Gwen. All right?"

He remained for a time on his knees, next to his dead friend. "Smiley," he said. "Dead."

"Yes," I said, "Smiley's dead."

He looked up at me and then back down at his friend.

I took him gently by the arm and together we walked back to the shelter.

25

On the way back from the airport, I told Donna what I'd learned. . . .

Richard was seven years old the day Karl finally deserted them. Richard never forgot how he'd held on to his father's pocket so hard that the pocket itself ripped out, infuriating Karl to the point where he bent down and slapped the boy hard across the mouth. The mother stepped in then and one of their terrible arguments ensued. No matter where Richard went in the three-room apartment he could hear arguing always; always. Cover his ears, bury his head; it made no difference. But on this day there was a special fury because this time his father had packed his bags and each of them knew he would be back no more. So Richard was on their bed when the front door was opened by the father and then slammed shut in rage by the mother, the father's footsteps already quick and retreating down the stairs.

Richard's mother died when he was eight. Heart disease. He was raised from then on by his aunt and uncle. He asked them constantly to try and find his father. But one day his uncle—his mother's brother—said, "If there's any justice, Richard, that sonofabitch died long before your mother did."

By rights, he should have hated his father. But
he could never quite bring himself to this. Even
later on when he escaped the factory neighborhood
of his aunt and uncle, when he was already riding
around in his first sports car and dating his first
rich woman, he still felt bereft and deserted, and
longed to see his father.

All this time, Karl was in California, seeking
those golden women and golden moments that the
sun and beach and starry nights seem to hold for
midwesterners in particular. He sought the work
he'd always sought—clothing salesman or car salesman or jewelry salesman—the sort of job where a
three-piece suit and a keen line of patter could hide
both poverty and relative ignorance. In 1973, when
he was forty-one years old, Karl had his first breakdown. He had no idea what it was about. After a
week of depression, he woke up in the middle of
the night and went into the bathroom and got a
double-edge razor blade and slashed his left wrist
into a little bleeding mouth. His woman at the
time—a cocktail hostess—got him to a psych ward.
Over the years, he would have more than sixty
electroshock treatments and remain institution-
alized for a total of more than ten years. Schizo-
phrenia was the easy, rote answer. In fact, the
shrinks could never quite agree about what trou-
bled Karl. He had good periods when he could
work and function well; but always the bad periods returned.

In 1988, during a good period, he phoned long

distance the woman who had raised Richard. He had never liked her—a Slav of almost desperate frugality and niggling meanness—and argued her into telling him where he could find Richard. So from California, he returned. He had little money and spent most of it on the Greyhound ticket. But somewhere in Wyoming he'd had another breakdown. The police, not knowing for sure what they were up against, took him off the bus in handcuffs as the other passengers gawked excitedly.

In one more year—another stay in a state hospital where the inmates shit themselves and the guards were known to rape the women—Karl came to the city where Richard lived.

By now of course Richard could not afford to see his father. His social circles were too refined. His father was too unpredictable. They had two meetings, one of which ended in rage (Richard screaming like a child about how bad his mother's last years were) and one in tears (Richard holding his father tightly and telling him again and again how much he loved him).

Karl then had another breakdown. Without realizing exactly what was wrong with him, Gwen took him into the shelter. He befriended Smiley and began to write his son threatening letters. He blamed his son's employees for the death of Smiley and that was why he began carving up his friend and serving him as communion. He did not seem to understand that Richard no longer cared about his social circle—that he wanted to go away and take his father somewhere and start again. But then Jackie killed him and it no longer mattered.

"So what's going to happen to Karl?" Donna asked after I told her everything Karl had told me after I'd taken him back to the shelter.

"Another institution. Probably permanent this time."

"I'm sorry, Dwyer. I wish I'd been here with you."

I smiled at Donna and leaned over and kissed her. We were in my bed in my little apartment and between us now was the kitten. Donna was going to take her home, saying she was a better mom than I was. About that I couldn't argue.

I lay back and thought about Richard and Karl. The kitty got on my chest and started nuzzling my jaw.

"Boy, does she like you," Donna said.

I laughed. "Boy, do I like her."

Donna leaned in and started scratching the kitty. "She's as crazy about you as I am, Dwyer."

The night wind rattled the windows and I wasn't sure why, but a great sorrow came over me then and for a time I could say nothing at all—just look at Donna and the kitty and feel how lucky I was and how unlucky Richard and his father had been.

Then I put the kitty in the chair and turned out the light and started to tell Donna how much I'd missed her.